UNSTEADY GROUND

LANTERN BEACH EXPOSURE
BOOK 3

CHRISTY BARRITT

River Heights

CHAPTER ONE

"I'LL BE HOME SOON," Ty Chambers murmured. "I promise."

Faith, his nineteen-month-old daughter, reached for him from her grandmother's arms. A cry teetered on the edge of her lips.

Ty's mom took a step back as she whispered reassuring words to Faith while bouncing the girl on her hip.

"She'll be fine," his mom insisted as she looked back at Ty, her short, dark hair freshly dyed and her oversized blue shirt blowing with the breeze. "You go to your meeting. I've already kept you for entirely too long."

His mom had gone on and on about how high her electric bill was this month. She was a talker, which was why Ty always allotted extra time when he came over.

With one more glance at Faith's big eyes, Ty stepped away.

Faith looked exactly like her mom, Cassidy, with her pert nose, expressive eyes, and wide smile. Her hair was blonde—although Cassidy's wasn't naturally that color. Apparently, it had been light-colored when she was younger.

As he stepped toward his house, which neighbored his parents' oceanfront cottage, he glanced at his watch.

Fifteen minutes. That's how long he had to make it to Blackout headquarters for his meeting.

Ty had cofounded the private security agency with his friend Colton Locke. The organization wasn't his only job. He also ran a nonprofit called Hope House, which helped injured military members recover from their time in service. He had another session starting in a few weeks, so his schedule would be busy as he nailed down all the details.

At least, the day was warm and balmy for early May. He was ready for the relatively cool spring to release its tight grip on the area.

He wanted to dive into the ocean waves again. To feel the saltwater against his skin. Maybe even to surf awhile before lying on the sand to dry off.

Those were some of his favorite things to do to unwind.

Ty headed toward his truck, parked beneath his stilted home, and started to open the driver's side door then paused.

Something on one of the wooden posts beneath his house caught his eye.

And caused his blood to turn ice cold.

Slowly, he walked across the sandy concrete slab.

He touched the red scarf tied around the post.

A red scarf that hadn't been there only fifteen minutes ago when he'd walked past this area with his daughter.

His spine stiffened as he glanced around.

Who had left this? The person appeared to be long gone.

Ty had a history with a red scarf. However, he never thought he'd see one again. Not like this. Not here on Lantern Beach.

As he scanned beneath his house and down the driveway beyond that, his gaze reached the dunes that protected the residence from the ocean.

He still didn't see anyone.

Ty stepped toward the dunes for a better look.

He climbed to the top and glanced around, halfway expecting to see someone running away or hiding behind some sea oats.

There was no one.

He spun around.

Even from his perch, he didn't see anyone on his driveway or on the road beyond it.

Back muscles still stiff, he scanned the six colorful cabanas built behind his home. He used them as part of Hope House, but they were empty now, and he kept them securely locked.

He slowly—cautiously—walked between them, looking for a sign that something was wrong.

Everything appeared untouched.

Whoever had left that scarf was no longer on his property.

Ty grabbed the scarf and tucked it in his pocket before walking back toward his truck.

He had security cameras installed around the perimeter of his house, but the area where that scarf had been tied was just out of range. The person who'd left it had probably been aware of the cameras and purposefully avoided them.

Just to be certain, Ty would check the recorded footage later.

Trouble from his past days as a Navy SEAL had followed him here.

His jaw tightened.

Now he had to figure out what to do about it.

Police Chief Cassidy Chambers stood on the shore of the Atlantic Ocean, not far from the Lantern Beach lighthouse.

Normally, she'd breathe deeply of the salty, fresh air and feel a burst of invigoration.

Not now.

Mayor Mac MacArthur stood on one side of her and Officer Braden Dillinger on the other. A few spectators, including the woman who'd called them, also lingered close.

Cassidy stared at the beach stretching before her and shook her head.

Hundreds of fish had washed ashore and lay dead on the sand. The aquatic graveyard probably stretched for more than fifty feet, maybe even closer to seventy.

Not only was the smell horrendous, but flies swarmed everywhere. Seagulls swooped in to feast on the buffet.

Mac stared at the sickly scene and shook his head. "What's strange is that the dead fish are all different kinds—mostly Spanish mackerel and flounder."

Cassidy squinted against the sun as it rose over the ocean and created a glare. "So that would indicate that this isn't some natural occurrence. It's most likely not the environment that killed them. Correct?"

Mac rubbed his jaw, gaze still fastened on the beach. "That's my best guess. But you're probably going to need to call the Wildlife Commission to check this out as well as the North Carolina Environmental Quality Agency."

"I'll do that. I'll have someone test the water too, just to make sure it's safe. Not many people go in the ocean at this time of year, but Memorial Day weekend is right around the corner. When that hits, tourists will flood here to enjoy the ocean. We have to make sure the water is safe."

"Yes, we do."

Cassidy turned toward Mac and studied his face, anxious for his wisdom right now. Mac had been the Lantern Beach Police Chief for decades and now served as mayor. He'd been around this area a lot longer than Cassidy had.

"You ever seen anything like this before?" Cassidy squinted against the early morning sunlight as it glinted off the ocean.

He ran a hand over the gentle wrinkles on his aging face. "On occasion, I've seen things like this happen. It's not always fish. Sometimes it's birds. Sometimes scientists can explain it, and sometimes they can't. I wouldn't get too concerned . . . not yet.

But we do need to have a sample of these fish checked out to be certain."

Cassidy couldn't agree more.

For now, she wanted to get away from this place before she threw up. The smell was *that* bad.

She turned to the crowd behind her. Spectators already had their phones out and were taking pictures and videos. People loved having something to talk about, to report to their friends on social media. This was feeding that urge.

She found the fortysomething woman who'd reported the fish. "Thank you for letting us know about this. We'll take care of the issue."

"I hope so." The woman frowned. "I hate seeing stuff like this. Seems inhumane, you know?"

"Sometimes, it's just nature," Mac piped in.

"And sometimes it's not." The woman lifted her brows as if unconvinced.

"I'm sure the state will investigate. Nobody likes this any more than you do."

Slowly, the crowd dispersed down the shore and toward the dunes to the walkover leading to the parking lot.

As they did, Cassidy's thoughts raced.

This fish kill . . . it didn't have anything to do with the new facility that had opened on the island . . . did it? Ocean Essence was a cosmetics lab that had opened here a couple of months ago. There was something about the company that Cassidy didn't trust.

The theory wouldn't leave her mind. She found it suspicious that an international cosmetic and skin-care company would open a facility on such an isolated, small island.

They said they'd come here for inspiration since their products were based on ingredients found in the sea. But Cassidy remained skeptical. She couldn't help but wonder if the company was hiding something.

She began to walk back to her police SUV.

She shouldn't jump to conclusions. She needed to do some research before she got tunnel vision that didn't allow her to see other possibilities. It was still possible that there was no crime here. That this was simply Mother Nature doing what Mother Nature sometimes did.

Cassidy paused at her SUV and turned toward Mac. "Let me know what the Wildlife Commission and NC Environmental Quality Agency says, please."

"I will. They'll probably want to test water quality at our ocean and sound beaches in accordance with federal and state laws."

"That's only wise."

"We can't have people swimming or playing in water with high bacteria levels—that can cause some nasty gastrointestinal illnesses and skin infections." Mac paused. "Anyway, if they do close the beach, I'll need you and your officers to post signs and spread the word."

"Of course." Cassidy nodded. "Just let me know what you need."

She glanced at the beach one more time.

She hoped this was just a crazy coincidence, a one-time thing that would be explained by some type of algae bloom or something.

But her gut told her that wasn't the case.

And her gut was usually right.

CHAPTER
TWO

MAKING A SPLIT-SECOND DECISION, Ty bypassed Blackout Headquarters and started driving down the road toward the police station instead.

He needed to talk to Cassidy.

Now.

But first, he called his parents and warned them to stay inside and lock the doors. Thankfully, they didn't ask too many questions, and Ty promised to explain more later.

Next, he called Colton.

His friend answered on the first ring. "What's going on?"

"Listen." Ty scanned the road around him, still looking for trouble. "I hate to cancel, but I had something come up. I can't make the meeting."

"Everything okay?" Concern captured his friend's deep voice.

"I hope so. I'll fill you in later. But for now, I can't make it."

"Okay, man. Let me know what I can do."

"I will." Ty ended the call.

He hoped it didn't come down to needing anyone's help. That this situation was simply a coincidence.

But he didn't think it was.

Danger was close.

He thought he'd felt someone watching him over the past couple of days. But every time he'd searched the area around him, he hadn't seen anyone.

Now he knew his instincts had been right. Someone *had* been watching him.

He sped down the road, traveling faster than usual. He needed to have this conversation with Cassidy face-to-face.

This part of his past—this mission—was supposed to be forgotten.

But here it was back again.

Cassidy and Faith's images flashed through his mind.

If Ravi Jabal had discovered Ty was here in Lantern Beach then Ty's family was in danger.

Only a handful of people knew about the significance of that red scarf. Only Ty, Daniel Oliver—who was now dead, Captain Rich Donaldson, and Jasmine Jabal. And now, possibly Ravi.

Ty's heart pounded harder as the thoughts collided in his mind.

He pulled into the police station parking lot at the same time as Cassidy. She climbed from her SUV and studied him a moment, clearly sensing his heightened emotions as he rushed toward her.

She raised her eyebrows and paused near her vehicle, pressing the button to lock it. A quick beep filled the air as she paced toward him. "I take it you're not here about today's fish kill?"

"I don't know anything about dead fish." He took her elbow and led her toward the door, not wanting to waste any time. "We need to talk. Somewhere private."

"You're scaring me."

He didn't bother to tell her she shouldn't be scared.

Because she should be. Ty could feel the danger thrumming through the balmy, salty air on the island.

"Let's go to my office." Cassidy's tense voice left no room for argument—and he knew better than to argue with her. His wife was smart, she had great instincts, and she was fiercely loyal.

Ty hated for Cassidy to feel apprehensive. But he

couldn't make light of this situation. The stakes could be life or death—her life and her death as well as their daughter's.

She led him inside and closed the door to her office. Then, without sitting down, she turned toward him.

Her intense, no-holds-barred gaze locked with his. "What's going on?"

———

Cassidy's pulse thrummed in her ears as she looked up at Ty and waited for his explanation.

"You might want to sit down." He nodded toward her leather office chair.

"I'm fine standing." She didn't want to waste another moment. She needed to know what had her tough-as-nails husband on edge. He was a former Navy SEAL. Nothing rattled him.

Except this.

That meant it was bad. Really bad.

And that fact had her stomach twisted in knots.

He stared at her a split second as if calculating what to say. "I think you and Faith could be in danger. I need to get you off this island to somewhere safe."

"Wait a minute . . . what?" she muttered.

Cassidy's thoughts raced, and she held up a hand —either to slow her own conclusions or to slow Ty's words. She wasn't sure. All she knew was that she couldn't breathe, especially at the mention of their daughter.

"What's going on, Ty?"

Ty drew in a long breath. Cassidy couldn't remember the last time she'd seen him look so burdened. Probably when a cult leader had almost killed her or when she'd been abducted right before giving birth.

He raked a hand through his spiky light-brown hair, and his eyes shifted back and forth as if computing his memories, his thoughts. His broad frame, usually one used to protect others, seemed tight and drawn. His blue eyes appeared troubled.

"Cassidy, ten years ago Daniel Oliver and I were sent on a special off-books assignment," he started. "We extracted—or rescued would be the more accurate term—the wife of the Sahili Empire's crown prince."

"What?" Her voice sounded wispy with confusion, even to her own ears.

"This woman—Jasmine—wanted to leave Ravi Jabal, but she was trapped. He was an evil man. He had multiple wives, but she was his favorite. He abused them all. Some died. Some disappeared never to be found again. Jasmine feared she'd be next."

"Okay . . ." Cassidy still wasn't following.

"In return for her rescue and a new identity, Jasmine offered up some valuable intel to the US government about a nuclear program Sahili was trying to launch. Because of her, we were able to shut that down. Ravi must have figured out what was going on. According to inside sources, he was furious. He vowed to catch the person or persons who helped her escape and have them beheaded."

"Beheaded?" Cassidy's throat went dry at his words.

That wasn't a method of death she heard mentioned very often. In all her years in law enforcement, she'd never worked a case involving that method of execution.

"In fact, Ravi killed three innocent people, thinking they'd helped her escape."

"That's terrible." She crossed her arms. "But I'm not sure why you're so concerned right now. You said that was ten years ago."

Ty's gaze flickered to the window as if he were worried that trouble may have followed him. "Cassidy, I haven't talked to Jasmine in ten years. The only people who knew about this mission were me,

Daniel, Jasmine, and Captain Rich Donaldson. No one else knew I was involved."

"Okay . . ." She tried to follow where he was going with this.

"Jasmine was gathering information for us in Ravi Jabal's palace. But as soon as she'd obtained the information we needed or when/if her life was threatened, she knew to put out a red scarf and we'd come. Any other type of communication was too dangerous."

"Wow. What happened after you rescued her?"

"We took her to a safe house in Paris." Ty's gaze locked with hers. "This morning, after I dropped Faith off with my parents, I came back to the house . . . and a red scarf had been tied around one of our posts."

He pulled the scarf from his pocket and placed it on her desk.

Cassidy's eyes widened as realization hit her. "So you think Jasmine is here in Lantern Beach?"

"Or Ravi found her, made her talk, and now he's here to get his revenge."

"Ty . . ." Her voice cracked.

He squeezed her hands. "That's why I need to get you and Faith off the island. I don't want something to happen to either of you."

Her thoughts continued to race. "Ty . . . I can't just leave."

"But you can't stay."

"The people here in town depend on me. I promised to serve and protect—not to abandon them at the first sign of trouble."

He squeezed her arm and stepped closer. "Cassidy, not only did Ravi behead his enemies, but he made them suffer through exsanguination first."

"Exsanguination?" Another method of death she didn't hear mentioned very often.

"He cuts his victims and lets them bleed out. Right before they die, he beheads them and hangs the head somewhere nearby to make a statement. He likes to call it the John the Baptist treatment."

Cassidy swallowed hard, trying to remain calm even as a tremor started deep inside her—especially when the image of her precious daughter filled her thoughts.

She'd brought a child into this world, knowing it was full of evil and suffering. Sometimes she wondered what she'd been thinking. If the decision had been cruel.

Cassidy had seen the worst sides of human nature. She knew what evil people were capable of. She knew what it was like to grieve, to hurt, to feel heartbreak.

Yet she'd also felt hope. She'd also desired change. She wanted to leave this world a better place than she'd found it.

She loved Faith with everything in her and would do whatever was necessary to protect her daughter. That started with keeping a level head. Thinking through things and not jumping to conclusions.

Cassidy drew in a deep breath, trying to remain calm. "We don't know that it's Ravi. What if it's Jasmine? What if she found you here?"

"Either way, if something were to happen to you or Faith . . ." Ty's eyes narrowed as if he fought back emotion.

Cassidy's heart lurched into her throat at the sight of his distress. Her husband was strong and self-assured. He wasn't the type to overreact.

She had already run from trouble once in her life. Had left behind everything and everyone she knew. She didn't want to do it again. Didn't want to upend everything because danger was closing in.

She now had a new name, a new look, and a new life away from the vicious gang that had wanted to kill her.

She wouldn't run again.

But then there was Faith . . .

She'd never forgive herself if something

happened to her daughter—especially if she had the opportunity to prevent it.

Cassidy's mind whirled until an idea formed. "See if your parents will stay at the Blackout Headquarters with Faith. They'll be safe there. We can assign them a guard 24–7, and we can stay there overnight too. Kujo also."

"I like that idea." Ty nodded slowly as that thought seemed to sink in. "But what about you? What are you going to do now?"

She mentally ran through everything she had to do. "I can't hide. I have a job to do. But I'll be careful."

"Cassidy." His head fell to the side, and he closed his eyes as if to hide his inner turmoil.

"This is what I do as police chief, Ty. You know that. I can't hide away at Blackout all day—especially not until we know something for certain."

He stared at her another moment before nodding. "You're right. Let me talk to my parents and get everyone set up at Blackout. In the meantime . . ."

"I'll be careful." Cassidy stepped closer, wanting to reassure him. "I'll see if there was any evidence left on the scarf, though I doubt there is. That material doesn't lend itself to fingerprints or anything of that sort."

"I checked it for hairs or other fibers and didn't

see anything. But I thought you might want to check it anyway."

"I will."

Ty leaned toward her and planted a long kiss on her lips.

"Promise me you will be careful. Because if something happened to you . . ." His voice caught, and he shook his head as if he couldn't finish that statement.

"I promise. Also, can you see what you can find out about Jasmine and Ravi? We need more answers before we make any big decisions."

He stepped back and nodded. "Already planning on it. But I'm going to make sure Faith is secure at Blackout first."

Cassidy nodded, trying to show more confidence than she felt.

Because, on the inside, fear nibbled away at her peace.

The life she'd built here in Lantern Beach couldn't wither and die like her life back in Seattle had . . .

But she knew all too well that it actually could.

CHAPTER
THREE

TY'S MOM and dad had asked a lot of questions when Ty insisted on taking them with Faith to stay at Blackout.

He told them he couldn't explain everything now.

He'd seen the concern cross their faces. They knew he'd faced danger as a SEAL. Knew there were things he couldn't tell them.

Right now, all he could think about was their safety.

Faith's safety.

He escorted the three of them, along with his golden retriever, Kujo, to headquarters himself. Helped them get settled into one of the apartments set up there for employees.

They would be fed and taken care of. A razor-wire fence surrounded the place, and no one got through the gate without passing by a guard first. Plus, the country's finest former special ops members lived there on campus, many with their wives and children.

This place had grown beyond his greatest expectations, and he was proud of the people who worked for him. They had leadership, integrity, and great work ethics.

Ty gave Faith a kiss on the head before turning to his parents, Del and Frank. He tried not to show just how tense he felt—but surely, they could read it on him. "I'll explain what I can when I can. Okay?"

"You've got me worried." His dad frowned as he studied him. "But you can count on us. We'll take good care of Faith."

"I know you will."

His mom had already been through so much with her cancer. She was in remission and living life to the fullest now. His parents had moved to Lantern Beach, staying there for part of the year to help with Faith, among other things. The rest of the time they spent traveling.

"Thank you. Cassidy and I really appreciate this."

With those words, Ty thanked his parents, kissed Faith again, and left. He didn't have time to waste.

He needed to talk to Colton and fill him in on these latest developments.

Then he needed to find out the latest intel on Ravi and if Jasmine was on the run.

Colton closed his laptop computer when Ty stepped inside and took a seat across from him in his downstairs office. The room had minimal decorations other than pictures of Colton's wife, Elise, and their baby.

"What's going on?" Colton's brow furrowed as he clearly anticipated whatever had Ty concerned.

Ty wasn't the type to overreact, and anyone who knew him knew that.

He gave his colleague a brief rundown on the situation—starting with the overseas rescue and ending with the red scarf he'd found this morning.

"The mission was top secret." Ty shifted in his seat as he wrestled with the ethics of what to say. "You can't tell anyone what I just told you."

"I understand." Colton nodded, his stony face hardening even more. "What does this woman look like?"

Using his phone, Ty went online, found an old picture of Jasmine, and showed it to Colton.

The woman was beautiful, with long dark hair, a heart-shaped face, and olive skin. She'd been a beloved royal back in her home country, dubbed The People's Princess by locals.

"I can keep my eyes open for her on the island,"

Colton said. "But how did she track you down here in Lantern Beach? And if she needs your help, why not just find you and talk instead of being cryptic? If your theory is right, it's going to be hard for you to offer any assistance if you don't know where she is."

"I've thought about all of that." Ty rubbed his ever-tightening jaw. "I'm not sure."

"And Ravi?"

"I can show you a picture of him, but he won't come here to do the preliminary work himself. He'll hire people. His men could look like anyone here. They'll blend in. And tourist season is close so we'll have more visitors here on the island, which will make everything harder."

"You mentioned preliminary work?" Colton's eyes narrowed with thought. "What do you mean by that?"

"Ravi likes to do the actual killing himself. I think he gets a thrill from it." Nausea gurgled inside him at the thought of how sick and twisted the man was.

Colton frowned. "We'll do whatever we can to help you."

"I need to keep my family safe."

"Of course. They'll be safe here."

Ty stood. "Right now, I need to make some phone calls. Last I heard, Jasmine was in France. But I don't know what happened in the years since I rescued her. I lost touch."

"Find out. Let me know what else I can do in the meantime."

———

Cassidy's mind still raced through everything Ty had told her when she was interrupted by a call from dispatch.

Suspicious activity had been reported at an empty house on the island.

Normally, this kind of call was something Cassidy sent one of her guys to check out. But given what Ty had just told her, she wanted to check this scene out herself.

Cassidy knew better than to go into a situation like that alone. To be safe, she'd take Officer Braden Dillinger with her.

Dillinger had worked with Ty in special ops. He was also married to one of Cassidy's best friends, Lisa, who owned The Crazy Chefette restaurant.

A few minutes later, she and Dillinger headed toward her SUV. The temperature was supposed to be in the mid-seventies today, with low humidity, and partly cloudy . . . in other words, perfect.

She paused when she saw the large black-and-white feather caught in her door handle. Weird.

It must have landed there from a bird flying overhead. Somehow, the sight of it felt like a bad omen—if she believed in those sorts of things.

She dropped it on the ground and climbed into her SUV to head to the residence.

"A neighbor saw some men at this house last night," Cassidy explained to Dillinger as she drove. "She said they didn't arrive until midnight, and they left around three a.m."

"So she thinks these men were breaking in?" Dillinger furrowed his brow.

"That's her theory. She said they didn't turn on any lights. Just used flashlights."

"Why'd she wait so long to call us?"

Cassidy gripped the wheel. "Apparently, not long after spotting the men at the house she lay down thinking she'd check again in a few minutes, but then she fell asleep. Her husband told her this morning that he got up in the middle of the night to use the bathroom. Heard someone over there. Looked out the window in time to see the men leave in the wee hours of the morning. So she thought she should be safe rather than sorry. See something, say something, you know?"

"That's the advice I always like to give."

A few minutes later, Cassidy and Dillinger pulled to a stop in front of a three-story teal-colored house located directly on the oceanfront. This was one of the nicer homes on the island, the ones that rented for nearly twenty thousand dollars during prime weeks.

Cassidy had settled a small domestic dispute at the house last summer. If she remembered correctly, there was a swimming pool complete with a lazy river in the back as well as amazing views of the Atlantic.

"Do we check out the house first or talk to the neighbors?" Dillinger asked as they stepped out.

Cassidy scanned the house. No cars were beneath it. She saw no signs anyone was here.

"Let's check the house out first," she said. "Then we'll see if any neighbors have security cameras that might have picked up any movement last night. It's doubtful since these are all rentals, but it can't hurt to ask."

Muscles poised for action, Cassidy climbed a flight of steps to the front door of the stilted home.

She twisted the knob.

It was locked.

She already had a keycode from the rental agency and confirmation that no one had rented the place this week.

Still, she hesitated before punching the code into the door.

She remembered what Ty had told her. She repressed a shudder as she pictured people being bled out and then beheaded.

Cassidy would be wise to keep that in the forefront of her mind. She had no firm reason to believe that was connected. But this was a small island . . .

She could be dealing with someone deadly. *Viciously* deadly.

With a glance at Dillinger, she punched the code in and pushed the door open.

A quiet house greeted them.

Regardless, she drew her gun.

Cassidy went to the left while Dillinger went right.

They'd cover the perimeter of each room, just to make sure no one was here and that nothing had been disturbed.

Like many homes on the beach, the first floor was all bedrooms. The floor with the grandest view was the living room—and that was usually the top level.

Cassidy paused in a coral-colored guest bedroom and spotted something sticking out from beneath the bed.

Pulling on a glove, she picked it up.

It was a picture of a boy, probably nine years old, with dark hair and a bright smile.

Had a past renter left this and the house cleaners missed it afterward?

It was a possibility. Either way, it didn't appear to be evidence.

Just in case, Cassidy tucked the photo into an evidence bag and then slipped it into her pocket before searching the rest of the house.

CHAPTER
FOUR

TY'S MUSCLES were taut as he arrived back home.

He'd been anticipating whatever trouble might be coming his way.

Had Jasmine left that scarf? Ravi? If so, why?

How would either of them even have found him?

This couldn't all be a coincidence, could it?

The questions tumbled through his mind.

As he entered the house, his gaze scanned the place. Everything appeared to be in place.

Feeling confident that his cottage was secure, he rushed to his office to check his security footage. He wanted to see if the cameras had picked up on anything.

But it was just as he thought—the scarf had been left just out of sight.

That meant someone was paying a lot of attention and knew where his cameras were located. Which areas the lenses would capture. Which areas to avoid.

He didn't like the thought of that.

He leaned back in his chair, the scent of the leather upholstery mixing with the aroma of the mints on the corner of his desk.

He still needed to find out more information.

He grabbed his phone and called the captain who'd authorized the mission to save Jasmine. Ty hadn't talked to his commander in years, and he wasn't even sure he'd be able to get through.

To his surprise, Captain Donaldson picked up on the second ring. The man, in his early sixties now, was a powerhouse. On the phone, he sounded much taller and broader than he actually was in real life. That was because his body could hardly contain his big personality.

Last Ty had heard, the man was getting close to retirement and had recently bought a new home on the Chesapeake Bay, far away from his office in Washington, DC.

"Ty Chambers . . . funny you called. I was just thinking of you." The man's steely voice came over the line.

Ty straightened in his chair, curious about his words. "Is that right?"

"What's going on?" Donaldson wasn't going to offer any more information—not without some more questions, at least.

"It's about Project Aladdin."

By the "hmm" Donaldson offered, Ty suspected his former captain knew something.

"Do you have any updates on the asset?" That's what they'd called Jasmine. Ty had to be careful what he said right now. This line should be secure, but he couldn't be certain.

"As a matter of fact, I do. Why are you asking?"

"Someone tied a red scarf outside my house today." Ty leaned back in his office chair as he waited for Donaldson's response.

Donaldson didn't answer right away, and the silence stretched.

Was the man shocked? Putting the pieces together?

"Something's come up, hasn't it?" Ty couldn't let this drop. "What do you know?"

A sigh sounded over the line. "About a week ago, Jasmine told her handler she was worried that she was being watched. We brought in two other men to check things out. We didn't want to move her if we didn't have to."

"Okay . . ."

"Three days later, her handler as well as one of

the new guards was found dead. The other guard, Agent Andrew Hurst, is still alive but barely. He's in ICU at the hospital, unable to communicate."

Ty's breath caught. "Were they cut?"

"Their heads were still attached, but they'd bled out." His voice sounded grim as he said the words.

This was getting worse and worse. "And the asset?"

"She's missing."

"Do you have eyes on The Executioner?"

"Of course, I do. But if he was able to grab her, he's too smart to bring her back to his palace. You and I both know that."

Ty couldn't argue. But if Ravi did have Jasmine hidden away somewhere, he could have gotten information out of her. Information about Ty.

His thoughts continued to race. "Was the asset still in Paris when this happened?"

"No, we'd moved her to Canada a year ago. Before that, she'd lived in numerous other places— mostly in Europe."

"Did she have any problems before the move?"

"Not specifically. But if we thought anyone was getting too close, we relocated her as a precaution."

Jasmine was more likely to be able to travel to Lantern Beach from Canada than from France. But he still had so many questions. "*Could* she be here in North Carolina?"

"It's entirely possible. Does she know your last name? I know the two of you were close."

Ty's spine tightened at the man's words. He quickly corrected, "We weren't close."

"She was fond of you."

"She was." More tension embedded itself between his shoulders. Assumptions could get people in trouble, and Ty had tried to squash the rumor mill a decade ago. Some of the gossip still lingered, obviously. "But she doesn't know my full name. I never told her."

"I'm sure she has ways of finding out. The Executioner would be able to track you down also. I'd operate with the utmost caution. He could have found you and sent his men there. Or she may have come looking for you because she felt safe with you." Undertones of accusation stained the captain's voice.

Ty ignored the silent allegations. He didn't like either scenario. "And if she did find me? What should I do?"

"Call me. I'll have my guys pick her up. If she did somehow manage to escape, The Executioner's men won't be far behind. If they grabbed her, he could even be using her to get to you. It's hard to tell at this point."

A bad feeling swirled inside him.

This was one whirlwind Ty had never intended on being pulled back into.

———

Cassidy cleared the first floor before she and Dillinger headed upstairs to the living room, kitchen, and master bedroom.

As soon as they cleared the staircase, a masked man lunged from behind a sofa across the room.

Immediately, Cassidy saw the gun in his hands. "Get down!"

He began firing, bullets splintering the stair railing beside them.

She and Dillinger both ducked into the closest room beside the staircase—the master bedroom.

Had this guy come back for something? Or had he stayed behind for some reason?

She had no idea.

Right now, she needed to concentrate on staying alive.

Cassidy gripped her gun and lifted a prayer.

Then she leaned out the door and took a shot.

The man was already running toward a sliding glass door—but not before firing more rounds at her.

This guy meant business.

In a break in the gunfire, she and Dillinger darted to the next closest wall—in the kitchen.

She couldn't let this guy get away.

Stepping out, she aimed at the man's retreating back.

"Stop right there!" she ordered. "Police!"

He stilled.

Raised his hands in the air.

"Drop your weapon!" Dillinger spoke up.

The next instant, the man spun around and raised his gun.

Cassidy's heart quickened as she pulled the trigger.

Dillinger fired a shot at the same time.

The bullets hit the man's shoulder. One embedded. One skimmed the flesh.

The man reared back upon the impact. He grunted but remained on his feet.

The next instant, he raised his gun again.

But not toward Cassidy.

Not toward Dillinger.

Instead, he shot the gas fireplace behind them.

"No!" Cassidy shouted.

The next instant, an explosion filled the room in a fiery rage.

CHAPTER
FIVE

THE BLAST THREW Cassidy and Dillinger to the floor.

Flames instantly licked the walls, the floor, the ceiling.

Smoke filled the space in a thick rolling fog.

Pushing herself up on her elbows, Cassidy glanced around. Dillinger stirred on the floor beside her, a dazed look in his eyes. Otherwise, he appeared okay.

She searched for an exit.

The stairs were blocked. The living room swallowed in flames.

The master bedroom. A house this size most likely had an exterior door leading to a deck. They could escape from there.

If only she and Dillinger could get to it before the flames did . . .

"We've got to get out of here!" Cassidy grabbed Dillinger's arm.

He rose to his feet just as Cassidy did.

"This way . . ." Cassidy pointed across the room.

They both darted toward the door. As they ran, Cassidy pulled out her radio and called in the incident. They needed the fire department here.

Now.

With flames crackling behind them, they sprinted through the bedroom, out a sliding glass door, and onto a wooden deck.

They needed to get as far away from the fire as they could.

Sucking in deep gasps of clean oxygen, Cassidy coughed, trying to clear her lungs. But she didn't stop moving. Not in this situation.

She grabbed onto the railing and sprinted down the stairs attached to the deck.

Only when she and Dillinger reached the driveway did Cassidy scan her surroundings, searching for any signs of the gunman who'd nearly killed them.

But he was nowhere to be seen.

How had he disappeared that fast?

Her throat tightened as another round of coughs erupted.

She glanced at Dillinger. He stood beside her, staring at the house, which was quickly becoming engulfed with flames. She felt the heat waves on her face. Heard crackling as the wood was consumed. Heard sirens in the distance.

She was so thankful they had gotten out when they did.

"Are you okay?" Cassidy asked her officer.

He pulled his gaze away and nodded. "I'm fine. You?"

"My ego's a little bruised, but that's about it."

"Did you recognize that man?" Dillinger's gaze remained on her.

"No. Did you?"

He shook his head. "No."

Cassidy's jaw hardened as the reality of the situation hit her. "I'm wondering if those men left someone here as a guard."

Dillinger nodded. "Maybe. But what was he guarding?"

"That's a good question." She pushed several stray hairs from her gaze as her thoughts raced.

"We might not ever find out. I'm afraid any evidence will be gone."

"Maybe that's why he caused the fire—not only

so he could get away but to conceal what they were doing there." As Cassidy said the words out loud, her gut twisted.

Was this connected with the incident Ty had told her about?

Considering how trouble seemed to find its way to Lantern Beach . . . there was a good possibility the answer to that question was yes.

———

Two hours later, Cassidy was still on the scene.

The fire was out, but the house had suffered a lot of damage.

Despite the grim situation, the sun still hung high and bright in the sky. Smoke filled the air directly around them, its sooty scent haunting them without escape.

Cassidy had talked to neighbors—including the ones who'd reported last night's intruders—but no one had seen where this guy had gone.

None of the nearby houses were equipped with security cameras, just as Cassidy had thought. Most vacation rental properties didn't have cameras for privacy purposes.

She'd also called Doc Clemson and asked him to keep his eyes open for any gunshot victims. So far, there had been none. But that man who'd been inside would need medical help.

He'd left a trail of blood that stopped at the driveway of a neighboring house. He must have stashed a car there, just out of sight.

Currently, firefighters continued to hose the house down, making sure no hot spots popped up. Occasionally, the spray drifted with the wind and wet Cassidy's face and hair.

Cassidy wasn't surprised when Mac had pulled onto the scene. He liked to stay abreast of what was going on here on the island. No doubt he'd been listening to the police scanner.

"Any idea who this guy was?" Mac met her in the driveway and handed her a cup.

She thanked him for the coffee and took a sip, grateful for the extra caffeine.

Cassidy would love nothing more than to share with her mentor what Ty had told her. But she couldn't do that. She'd promised Ty she'd keep the details quiet.

Still, Cassidy didn't like secrets. She'd kept so many for so long when she'd first moved to the island under an assumed identity. She didn't want to hide anything now. Especially not from Mac.

"No leads yet," she finally said. "Just trying to figure out what's going on here."

Mac stared at the house and took a sip of his own coffee. "You and me both."

Cassidy's thoughts continued to race. "This guy must have been using incendiary bullets. It's the only way he could have ignited the fumes in the fireplace and caused an explosion."

"I was thinking the same thing. Those bullets are no joke."

"You've got that right," Cassidy muttered.

Mac nodded at the home in front of them. "Such a shame about this house. It was beautiful."

Her jaw tightened. "Yes, it was."

The property manager would let the homeowner know, but Cassidy knew this would be a devastating loss for them.

She couldn't help but wonder if it was her fault. Or Jasmine's. Or Ty's.

She wasn't sure. But she felt certain the men who'd been here might be connected with that red scarf Ty had found.

Her spine felt pinched with tension at the thought.

She didn't want these people anywhere near Faith. The thought of it . . . well, it was her worst nightmare.

Cassidy felt Mac studying her and forced herself to keep a neutral expression. The man could read her a little too well. She decided to change the subject to avoid any more lies.

She cleared her throat and took another sip of her coffee. "Any updates on the fish kill?"

"Someone from the state should be arriving by tonight. But more fish washed up in that same area by the lighthouse."

"What is going on?" The whole thing just seemed so strange. In Cassidy's mind, things like deadly algae blooms happened in warm months. But she was no biologist.

"Hopefully, they'll be able to figure it out." Mac twirled a pencil between his fingers. "For now, we should keep a close eye on the beaches and be ready to close them if we need to."

"I agree. We have to keep people safe. I know how the surfers around here are. As soon as they think the swells are good, nothing is going to stop them from trying to catch a big one." Cassidy waved away a piece of ash floating past on the wind.

But her words rang in her ears—*we have to keep people safe*.

Was that even possible?

Or had trouble unlike they'd ever known come to her precious Lantern Beach?

CHAPTER
SIX

TY STEPPED onto the screened-in porch outside his front door to get some fresh air and figure out a plan of action.

Donaldson hadn't given him anything solid to go on as far as where Jasmine might be.

But the fact two members of her detail were dead, Ravi style, set all kinds of alarms off in his head.

In other circumstances, Ty would assume Ravi had grabbed her.

But if that was the case, then how had the scarf gotten here?

What if Ravi was setting Ty up? If so, for what?

Ty's head pounded, and even the fresh ocean breeze couldn't cure his problems now. He closed his eyes and lifted up a prayer for everyone's protection.

Then, before he forgot about it, he texted his Bible study group.

They were supposed to meet at the house tonight, and it wasn't safe for anyone to come here. He told them next week should still be good.

He hoped that would be the case, that this wouldn't stretch on too long and that they could nip it in the bud.

Right now, he wanted to check in with Cassidy, to see how she was doing. She was trained, smart, and capable.

But he still worried.

If these guys had murdered highly trained government agents, then they could get to anyone.

He grabbed his phone from his pocket to make the call.

But before he dialed her number, movement at the edge of the house caught the corner of his eye.

In two seconds flat, his gun was drawn and pointed. "Who's there?"

He braced himself, anticipating one of Ravi's men.

Instead, a woman stepped up the outside stairway, her hands in the air.

"Please, don't shoot." Her voice, stiff with broken English, trembled with fear.

Ty lowered his weapon as surprise washed through him. "Jasmine?"

She *had* found him. But was she alone?

Was Ravi setting all this up?

Ty remained alert to his surroundings as he glanced at her.

The slender woman hadn't aged much in the ten years since he'd seen her last. Her dark hair was a little thinner and the circles beneath her eyes more defined. Instead of dressing like royalty, she wore skinny jeans, a black sweatshirt, and running shoes.

Her big eyes met his. "I didn't know where else to go."

A million questions rushed through his head as he continued checking to see if trouble had followed her here.

He saw no one.

"Are you here alone?" He needed to hear the words come from her lips.

"Of course." Jasmine quickly nodded.

Ty gestured toward his front door. "Let's get you inside where it's safer."

He glanced behind him one more time before ushering Jasmine into his house.

She was alive. That was the good news.

The bad news?

Trouble wouldn't be far behind.

———

Cassidy needed to see Ty.

Needed to decompress.

Needed to ask more questions.

As soon as she could, she left for the day and started toward Blackout. But when she checked the Friend Finder app on her phone, she saw Ty was at home.

She headed that way instead.

Her head throbbed, and she knew she might need to go back to work tonight.

More than anything, she wanted to see Faith. To hold her sweet daughter. To smell her freshly shampooed hair and feel the toddler's soft skin beneath her fingers.

For now, that would have to wait.

First, she needed to talk to her husband.

Cassidy pulled into her driveway, noting Ty's 1958 teal Chevy truck was there.

Her muscles remained tight with caution as she walked up the stairs toward the front door.

She had to remain on guard, whatever she did. Being caught by surprise could be deadly.

She reached the front door and inserted the key.

But the door was already unlocked.

Strange.

Ty never left the door unlocked.

Had something happened?

Was someone else here?

Quietly, Cassidy pushed the door open with one hand, the other hand hovering over her holstered weapon.

As her living room came into view, she spotted two people standing together in the center of the space.

Ty . . . and a woman whose arms were wrapped around his neck.

Cassidy gasped first but then outrage filled her.

This wasn't the kind of danger she'd been expecting.

But it was a danger, nonetheless.

Ty quickly pushed the woman away and turned toward Cassidy, his voice almost flustered—which was so unlike him.

"This isn't what it looks like," he rushed.

The woman frowned and stepped back before observing Cassidy with open disdain.

The woman was beautiful. More than beautiful. She was drop-dead gorgeous.

And she'd been embracing Ty.

Cassidy wasn't normally the jealous type, but a surge of . . . something raced through her. She couldn't quite identify the emotion—or maybe she didn't want to.

"Cassidy, this is Jasmine. Jasmine, this is my wife, Cassidy." Ty ran a hand through his hair, looking disheveled. Even his breaths seemed to be coming quickly, like they were too shallow.

Cassidy trusted her husband. She truly did.

But she didn't like this whole scenario, and she still wasn't sure what was going on here.

One thing was certain.

She would be finding out.

CHAPTER
SEVEN

TY NEVER PANICKED.

Until now.

As soon as he and Jasmine had stepped inside, Jasmine had thrown her arms around him. She'd wept into his shoulder.

He'd tried to pull her hands from around his neck.

Then Cassidy had walked in.

He was thankful for a level-headed wife, but he would definitely get an earful about this. He couldn't blame her.

Cassidy still stood near the door glancing back and forth between the two of them, her gaze discerning but cold.

"You were the only one who could help," Jasmine

started as she turned back toward Ty. "I had nowhere else to go."

She started to reach for him again, but he stepped away, his back stiff.

"How'd you find me, Jasmine?" He kept his voice all business.

"I read an article about Hope House. I saw your picture. So I stored away that information in case I ever needed it. It was a good thing. Because I need you now, Ty."

"Maybe we should all sit down." Cassidy's voice had an almost icy tone to it.

"Good idea." More heat crept up Ty's cheeks—not because he was guilty. But because that scene back there had made him all kinds of uncomfortable.

They went to the dining room, awkward tension stretching through the air.

In other circumstances, he'd offer to make coffee or tea.

Right now, he didn't want to take the time. Instead, he grabbed some water bottles and set them on the table. They would have to do for now.

He took a seat at the dining room table next to Cassidy and across from Jasmine. He didn't miss Jasmine's slight pout at his decision. At one time, he'd found the expression endearing. Not any longer. Now it seemed almost manipulative.

"I thought they relocated you to Canada?" He kept his voice level, determined to keep the proper boundaries in place.

Jasmine's eyes lit. "You've been keeping up with me?"

Ty kept his voice reserved. "Not until today. When I found that scarf, I decided to make some calls."

"I figured you would. That's why I left it there for you to find." She nodded, her eyes darting about the room anxiously.

"Why didn't you just knock on the door?" Cassidy asked. "Why leave the scarf?"

It was a good question, but Jasmine chose to ignore it.

"I was in Canada. Ravi's men tried to capture me there. If they did, they would have taken me back to him. But . . . I got away."

"How did you end up here?" Ty asked.

"Ravi's men . . . they found out where I was living. I drove away before they could catch me. Then I kept driving until I got here. I didn't know where else to go."

"Didn't the government assign you to someone?" Cassidy crossed her arms, obviously skeptical. "A handler or someone to contact in case things went south?"

Jasmine looked at Ty, a touch of surprise in her gaze. "She knows about me?"

Ty wasn't sure if Jasmine was flattered or offended that he'd told Cassidy any details. Maybe a little of both—flattered because he'd talked about her, offended because he'd opened up to someone else about her.

"Yes, she knows," Ty admitted.

Jasmine's eyes narrowed as her thoughts seemed to shift. "I had a handler, but Ravi found me somehow. Ravi killed Stanley. I didn't know what to do or where to go. I didn't know who I could trust besides you."

"Did anyone follow you here?" Cassidy's voice remained all business.

Something about her tone made Ty think there was more to her question than she let on. Did something else happen here on the island today?

He didn't ask. Not now.

"I'm not sure." Jasmine sucked in a breath, appearing to pull back more tears as her expression tightened.

The woman had hardened in the years since Ty had known her. Gone was much of her innocence. If Ty had to guess, she'd learned to be conniving during her time in hiding. It was a survival mechanism, he supposed.

"What do you mean, 'you're not sure' if anyone followed you here?" Cassidy tilted her head as she observed the woman. "I would think you'd be hyper-vigilant about not being followed."

Jasmine gave Cassidy a half eye roll, then her gaze locked with Ty's. Her lips trembled. "Oh, Ty . . . I don't know anything anymore—not for sure. Other than the fact if Ravi's men find me again . . . and if they capture me, I'll be dead!"

———

Cassidy didn't like this woman.

She wasn't sure if it was because Jasmine was clearly attracted to Ty or if it was because Cassidy thought the woman was lying.

Either way, Cassidy's shoulders were so tense that they physically ached.

As Ty and Jasmine continued to talk, Cassidy paced toward the window.

If trouble had followed Jasmine, Cassidy wanted to know. She needed to be ready to act.

"Start from the beginning." Ty's jaw visibly hardened as he stared at Jasmine. "When did you first know Ravi's men had found you in Canada?"

"I saw them following me one day as I was coming home from the store."

"How did you know for certain it was them?" Ty asked. "Did you recognize them?"

A flash of defiance flittered through her gaze. "I didn't know any of them if that's what you're asking. It was just . . . there was something in their eyes. These men may have looked normal, but they weren't. It's hard to pinpoint what it was exactly. Maybe a gut feeling. But I can spot Ravi's guys a mile away."

Cassidy believed in intuition, so she couldn't argue with the woman's words.

"What happened then?" Ty shifted as he leaned across the table toward Jasmine.

Jasmine seemed to eat up the attention from Ty. She sat up straighter, and her eyes brightened.

"I went back to my place. I tried to call my protection detail. They were staying right across the street. But my phone was jammed. I wasn't sure if it was because service was down—that did happen sometimes—or because someone had blocked my signal."

"Did you put up the scarf?" Ty asked.

"I did, but they didn't respond. So I grabbed my things and snuck out in the middle of the night." Tears filled Jasmine's eyes. "I stopped by to tell them what was going on. But one was already dead. Then I really panicked. I managed to make it to my car. I started driving and didn't look back."

"And you came here?"

She used the sleeve of her sweatshirt to wipe beneath both her eyes. "That's right. I've been trying to keep up with you. I read an article about this Hope House that you've started, so I came here to find you. However, when I arrived, I wasn't sure how to approach you."

"Where have you been staying on the island?" Cassidy stared at Jasmine.

"I don't have much cash with me, so I found someone willing to let me stay on their boat." Jasmine raised her chin as if anticipating that Cassidy would second-guess her decision. "This man and his girlfriend seemed trustworthy, like they wanted to help. I didn't know what else to do."

Jimmy James Gamble and Kenzie Anderson . . .

It had to be them. They were the only ones on the island who fit that description.

"How did you even get here from the marina?" Ty asked.

"I drove. I parked down the road and walked from there. I didn't want to draw any attention. I mean, other than your attention, Ty. Which is why I left the red scarf for you to find." Her wide eyes latched onto Ty's, tears brimming in them.

Ty didn't seem to notice. He'd gone into work mode as he tried to figure out the best plan of action.

For some reason, that caused Cassidy to feel immense relief.

"We need to get you in touch with someone who can relocate you to a safe place." Ty nodded as if the decision was foregone.

"No! We can't tell anyone I'm here. I'm afraid someone in your government works for Ravi. Think about it. It's the only way Ravi's men would have found me." Jasmine's gaze latched onto Ty's, desperation swimming in the depths of her dark brown eyes.

Cassidy didn't want to believe Jasmine. But the woman had a point.

How *would* she have been made otherwise?

As Cassidy's thoughts continued to churn, she glanced out the window again. The darkening beach stared back—but nothing else. No other signs of trouble.

Not yet.

"I didn't know where to go or who to turn to . . . you're the only person who came to mind." Jasmine implored Ty with her gaze. "You saved my life once. I hoped you would be willing to do it again."

Ty exchanged a glance with Cassidy.

Cassidy couldn't shake the suspicion she felt. Jasmine might be in trouble, but there was something the woman wasn't telling them.

And she was trying to use her feminine wiles to convince Ty to help.

That sent up major red flags in Cassidy's mind.

"Can the two of us talk in private a moment, Ty?" Cassidy asked.

"Of course." Ty stood and glanced back at Jasmine. "Help yourself to any food in the kitchen. And stay away from the windows, just to be safe. Okay?"

Jasmine nodded, but her expression remained forlorn and anxious—and possibly a touch rejected.

Cassidy and Ty went to Ty's office.

Though Cassidy wasn't entirely comfortable leaving Jasmine alone in her home, she had no choice.

"That wasn't what it looked like," Ty started as they paused just inside the room near the door.

"I know. I trust you." Cassidy's shoulders and neck felt tight—really tight, but she couldn't relax right now. "What do you plan to do?"

"I can't leave Jasmine on her own. If Ravi's guys find her . . ."

Cassidy drew in a deep breath. "We can't take her to the Blackout Headquarters, not until we know we can trust her."

Ty narrowed his eyes. "You think she's making this up?"

"I really don't know. There are some holes in her story, though."

"People can do strange things when they panic."

Cassidy frowned. "I don't like the sound of any of this. And I don't like the idea that trouble might have followed her here—followed her to you. She can't stay with us, not with Faith. I don't want her anywhere near our daughter."

"Then what should we do?" Ty's gaze locked with Cassidy's as he waited for her answer.

"I know one thing for sure—she can't stay here at our house with you guarding her while I'm with Faith." Her tone turned sharper than she'd intended. "That won't be happening."

"Cassidy . . ."

She shook her head, feeling adamant about her statement. "Look, maybe you don't have feelings for Jasmine, but she *clearly* has feelings for you. I can tell by the way she looks at you."

Ty didn't disagree. "I know that her staying here wouldn't be a good idea—especially not alone with me. But what's an alternative? The inn in town wouldn't be safe. Blackout is the only other place."

Cassidy crossed her arms, feeling entirely more defensive than she should. Yet she couldn't shake it either—and maybe she shouldn't.

"Faith is at Blackout," Cassidy said. "Your

parents. Our friends. We can't invite danger onto the campus."

Ty sighed and looked into the distance. Cassidy gave him a moment to think this through.

Finally, their gazes met again, and Ty said, "I can't just send her on her merry way to fend for herself. If she goes back to the boat, Jimmy James and Kenzie would be in danger. She doesn't have anyone else, and she risked her life to come here."

"And now that she's here? *Our* lives are at risk."

He sighed and raked a hand through his hair. "I'm sorry. I don't know the best way to navigate this."

Cassidy tried to think of another solution but came up with nothing.

Was there an ideal resolution for this situation?

She wasn't sure.

But she wouldn't stop trying to find one.

CHAPTER
EIGHT

TY RAN a hand over his face as he tried to decide the right course of action.

He had to do what was best for his family. But he couldn't pretend Jasmine wasn't part of this situation, like she didn't exist.

"I don't want to be in this position." He took Cassidy's hand and squeezed it. "But I can't look the other way either."

"I understand. That's what I love about you—you're always thinking of others." Compassion filled Cassidy's gaze as she nodded at the office door. "Let's go talk to Jasmine some more. Then maybe we'll be able to figure out a solution."

As a united front, they stepped out to talk to Jasmine.

But when they reached the kitchen, she was gone.

Alarm raced through Ty.

"Maybe she's in the bathroom." Cassidy was already moving down the hall to check it out as she said the words. She paused by the bathroom and frowned. "She's not in there."

Cassidy continued down the hallway, looking in each room.

As she did, Ty rushed upstairs and searched the rooms there.

They were empty.

Jasmine wasn't inside the house.

Ty and Cassidy met in the kitchen at the same time and without saying anything headed toward the door.

Ty paused when he reached it.

A smear of blood stretched across the white frame.

His heart pounded harder.

Had someone taken Jasmine in the brief amount of time he and Cassidy were talking?

He burst outside and scanned the darkening beach around him.

But he saw no one.

He and Cassidy had probably only talked for five minutes. Could Jasmine really be that far away now? It didn't seem possible. He hadn't heard anything—and he'd been trained to listen for trouble.

"We can check the security footage," Cassidy suggested.

"I'm afraid we don't have time for that right now. Jasmine will be long gone."

"She probably already is." Cassidy rubbed her neck as if her muscles were tight. "Do you think something spooked her?"

Ty started to shrug when something in the distance caught his eye. He nodded at a car pulling down the long gravel driveway toward the house. "Maybe."

Cassidy withdrew her gun. "One of Ravi's men?"

"I have no idea. Maybe Jasmine somehow got word someone was on their way." Ty would have to make sense of this later.

For now, they braced themselves for whatever was about to happen.

————

Cassidy watched as a man she'd never seen before stepped from the car.

He didn't look armed—or dangerous.

But she wouldn't let down her guard.

"Can I help you?" Ty called down from the deck.

"I'm looking for Ty Chambers." The thirtysomething man—dressed in business casual—stared up at them. He had a ruddy complexion, thick light-brown hair, and an air of propriety about him.

"Why are you looking for Ty Chambers?" Ty's voice contained an edge of caution.

The man grinned as if totally at ease. "I'd like to hire him."

Cassidy and Ty exchanged a look.

"And who are you?" Cassidy stared at the man, not bothering to hide her scrutiny.

"Rex Houghton. I'm in need of protection."

This day was just getting better and better, wasn't it? All Cassidy wanted to do was to see her sweet daughter. To talk to Ty alone. To regroup before returning to work tomorrow.

It appeared none of that would be happening.

Ty walked down the exterior stairs to meet the man. As he did, Cassidy scanned their surroundings one more time.

There was no sign of Jasmine. Since no one was supposed to know the woman was on the island, it wasn't as if Cassidy could ask around about her.

She hoped Jasmine was okay. Though she had a bad first impression, Cassidy didn't wish any harm to come to the woman.

Only when Cassidy felt certain danger wasn't lurking in the marsh grasses or behind the dunes did she join Ty in the driveway. But her muscles felt triggered, ready to act if necessary.

She hoped it didn't come to that.

"I'm with Retro Tech," Rex said as Cassidy stepped downstairs. "We're a state-of-the-art company that develops innovative AI technology."

Cassidy had heard of the company—and of the man, now that he mentioned it. She'd heard Rex planned to come to Lantern Beach, and she'd been dreading his visit.

She'd researched the man when she'd first learned he'd be coming here.

His presence would most definitely cause a headache here on the island.

He wanted to start a Think Tank on Lantern Beach.

Like the town needed something else to stir up trouble.

Again, she had to wonder, why Lantern Beach?

Residents weren't going to like another new business moving in.

She'd dealt with protests before. Some people wanted more development. Others wanted less. Some thought animals needed more space and that humans shouldn't encroach. Others thought people were always the priority.

She'd heard the same debate time and time again.

Always with no clear resolution.

"Why do you need protection?" Ty crossed his muscular arms over his chest, his stance making it clear he wasn't someone to be messed with.

"I've made a lot of enemies in my lifetime." A frown flickered across Rex's face. "A lot. And I'm afraid one of them might try to kill me someday."

CHAPTER
NINE

"WHY HAVE you made a lot of enemies?" Cassidy stepped closer, curious about the man's answer.

"My company can be unconventional at times in getting people's attention." Rex shrugged. "We need to open people's eyes and make them aware of things they may not see otherwise."

"Is that why you're in Lantern Beach now?" Her voice came out more accusatory than she'd intended.

Rex let out a nervous laugh. "I mean no harm here. I'm looking to move somewhere I can host retreats with certain people in my company—much like you do for Hope House, yes?"

He knew about Hope House, huh? The man had done his research. She wasn't sure if she was impressed or disturbed.

"And this is a wonderful island," Rex continued.

Cassidy felt certain there was more to his story. His answer seemed vague and too tidy.

"You said you've made a lot of enemies." Ty's jaw flexed as he observed the man with a measured glance. "Anything specific happen that you're talking about right now?"

Rex's face went taut. "As a matter of fact, yes. I was hoping I'd left trouble behind when I came here to the island. I've been here four days, just to let you know. But I've mostly been resting. When I stepped out my front door this morning, this was sitting right there on the porch."

He held up his phone to show them a picture.

Cassidy frowned when she saw it. "It looks like a bowl of . . . blood."

"I don't believe the blood was real." Rex's lips twitched as if he wanted to frown. "I saved the liquid at my house. It smells like cherry syrup."

"That had to be unsettling," Ty muttered.

Rex shrugged. "I'm used to getting threats. But this one was unusual, to say the least."

Cassidy stepped closer. "Why didn't you tell the police right when this happened?"

He raised an eyebrow as if surprised she knew it hadn't been reported. "Who says I didn't?"

"I do." She flashed her badge. "I'm the police chief."

His eyes widened. "I see. A power couple. I like it."

Cassidy didn't give him the pleasure of responding to his statement. Instead, she asked, "Are you here because of Ocean Essence?"

Something flickered in Rex's gaze. "Why would you think that?"

"The timing is uncanny."

He said nothing.

That was answer enough for Cassidy.

She'd had her eye on the lab for a while, wondering if the company was doing anything unethical.

Maybe they were.

Rex looked back at Ty, determination locking into his gaze. "I'm willing to pay."

If Cassidy remembered correctly, this guy had made good money in the tech field before starting this new company.

"This isn't usually the way we do things." Ty's intense gaze remained on the man.

"I couldn't get onto the Blackout Headquarters to hire someone." Rex shrugged. "I tried to call and left a message."

"It can take us up to twenty-four hours to call back," Ty told him. "How did you know to come here then?"

That was an excellent question, Cassidy mused.

"People on the island told me about you, so I tracked you down. I mean no harm. You must understand—I'm desperate. I've felt as if someone is watching me. The bowl of blood seems to confirm it. I fear the next course of action will be . . ." He swallowed hard before finishing. "Will be murder. My murder."

Maybe he was desperate. But Cassidy didn't quite trust this guy either.

Was she simply becoming cynical after being in her line of work for this long?

Or did she have a good reason to feel this way?

She wasn't sure. She had too much going on to think clearly.

Ty got Rex's number.

He needed to talk to his guys. See if anyone was available. Their calendar had been slammed—and he wanted to keep a detail on Faith as well.

Even though she was at the Blackout Headquarters, he couldn't take any chances.

When Rex pulled away, Cassidy turned toward Ty. Exhaustion was written on her face—in the slight circles beneath her eyes, in her hair as it slipped from its bun, in her shirt as it came untucked.

Ty knew she'd been trying to juggle so much lately. He tried to ease as much of the burden as he could. But her job was demanding. *Motherhood* was demanding.

"I need to tell you about what happened today." The quiet, serious tone to Cassidy's voice made it clear this was a big deal, not a conversation about something casual.

He glanced around, checking for trouble before nodding above them. "Let's go inside."

She squeezed his arm. "Better yet—let's go to Blackout. I'll talk as I drive. I need to see Faith."

"Understood. I'll lock up."

A few minutes later, they were in Cassidy's SUV. She told Ty about the break-in, intruder, and explosion.

"You think Ravi's men are behind it?" he asked.

"I'm not sure. We don't have any leads so far."

"These guys who were in that house . . . they had to go somewhere when they left."

"My guys are out there looking. But the neighbor said they were very quiet and sneaky."

He squeezed her hand. "You could have been hurt. I'm so glad you're okay."

"Me too." Cassidy frowned as she stared at the

gray, twilight-filled road ahead. "But this is far from being done."

A frown tugged at his lips. "I know."

"We need to figure out what happened to Jasmine."

"We do. Should we go to the marina? See if she went back there? Or if we can confirm she was staying on the boat where Jimmy James and Kenzie are working maybe we can find some kind of clue in her belongings—if she left any."

"Great idea."

"Do you still want to see Faith first?" Ty stole a glance at her as if trying to read her expression.

Cassidy frowned. "I do. But we need to figure out if Jasmine is in danger. I know Faith is safe and being loved on by Grammy and Pawpaw."

"It's your decision." Ty didn't pressure her, knowing she didn't need any more of that in her life.

With a resolute nod, she looked straight ahead. "Let's go to the marina. I have a sinking feeling we need to get to the bottom of this before things escalate."

CHAPTER
TEN

CASSIDY DIDN'T LIKE to question herself. But she was doing just that right now.

Maybe she should forget about this. Go to the Blackout Headquarters. See Faith.

But it was her duty to protect the people on this island. And, like it or not, Jasmine was on this island. Her very presence might put others in danger.

Cassidy remembered the smear of blood on the doorframe.

Jasmine might be in danger also.

The sooner she could put an end to this situation, the better.

The two of them pulled to a stop in front of the dark marina. During the day, the place was bustling with fisherman and charter boat tours. But right now, all was quiet.

Only a few boats on the island were large enough to have a room for Jasmine to rent. *Diamond of the Seas*, the boat Captain Jimmy James and Kenzie worked on, was one of those.

How had the woman even thought to do this? There was still so much that didn't make sense to Cassidy. But she tried to hold her opinions at bay—at least, until she had more information.

"You want to see if we can find Jimmy James and Kenzie?" Ty shifted toward her as they sat in the SUV.

She nodded. "Yes, let's do that."

She wasn't the jealous type. But there was something about Ty's protectiveness of Jasmine that made her emotions feel wound a little too tightly.

Cassidy would get over it. She knew she would. The initial shock of everything—along with exhaustion—was getting to her.

She and Ty walked along the docks before coming to a stop in front of *Diamond of the Seas*, a super yacht that almost looked out of place here at the rugged harbor.

They arrived just in time to see Jimmy James and Kenzie step off and head down the slip hand in hand.

The two smiled when they spotted Ty and Cassidy.

"What brings you by?" Jimmy James paused in

front of them, wearing cutoff jean shorts and a black T-shirt. He clearly wasn't on duty. "Nothing good, I'm assuming."

Jimmy James was a reformed bad boy. He'd been in a lot of trouble in his younger days, but he'd turned his life around. Meeting Kenzie, who was now his fiancée, had helped solidify that decision.

Yet, to look at the man, Cassidy could see why someone would be frightened of him. Not only was he tall and muscular, but he had multiple tattoos and an overall rough look about him. Despite that, he had a good heart, and Cassidy liked him.

She was rooting for him to stay on the straight and narrow, and he had for a long time now. Kenzie had helped immensely with that. The woman was good for him, no doubt.

"Do you have anyone staying on your boat?" Ty nodded at the yacht beside them.

The smile disappeared from Jimmy James's face as he went still. "Why would you ask that?"

Cassidy lowered her voice. "We believe she's in danger."

"Is that right?" A trepid looked filled Kenzie's face as her gaze went still.

"Look, we know there's a good chance that if someone is staying here, she's asked you to keep it quiet," Ty said. "We understand that. But we need to find her."

Jimmy James rubbed his neck, hesitating still.

Cassidy would give him another few minutes until she played hardball with him.

They needed answers—now.

Because with every second that passed, danger grew.

———

Ty's patience was running thin today, and he struggled to keep it in check. Losing it wouldn't help the situation. But the pressure cooker he was in continued to crush him.

"She was staying here." Jimmy James flicked his shoulders up in a quick shrug. "She asked us not to tell anyone."

Finally, some answers. A brief wave of relief swept through Ty.

"Did she tell you why?" Cassidy asked.

Jimmy James rubbed his jaw as if he wasn't comfortable with the conversation. "She said she needed privacy and that some bad men were after her."

"How did she even find you?" Ty wasn't sure if that detail was important or not, but he wanted to know, maybe for his own sake.

"We were leaving for the night, probably three days ago." Kenzie's hands went to her narrow hips as she recalled the story. "I saw someone behind the marina office. At first, I thought it was a teenager. Then this woman stepped out. She seemed frightened."

"How so?" Cassidy asked.

Kenzie nibbled on her bottom lip a moment before answering. "I don't know exactly. Just her whole demeanor, I guess. The way she kept glancing around. It was clear something was wrong. I asked if I could help her, and she said she was looking for somewhere to stay on the down low."

"So you offered her a room on the yacht?" Ty asked. "That seems risky considering how much the boat is worth and how much damage a stranger could potentially do."

"There was something about her that made us want to help." Jimmy James shrugged. "Mary—that's what she told us her name was—seemed desperate. We've been monitoring her to make sure she's on the up-and-up. So far, so good."

Cassidy found a picture of Jasmine on her phone. "Is this Mary?"

Jimmy James and Kenzie leaned closer for a better look before they both nodded.

"That's her," Kenzie said.

"Are you sure?"

"One hundred percent."

"When did you see Mary last?" Cassidy asked.

Kenzie glanced at Jimmy James and shrugged. "I don't know . . . two hours ago maybe."

Jimmy James nodded toward a grove of trees at the edge of the marina. "That's where she parked. Her car is gone now. It was a black sedan. A Nissan, I think."

"Thank you." Cassidy stepped back toward the docks. "I appreciate you sharing."

"I hope she's okay." Kenzie looped her arm through Jimmy James's. "I don't know what's going on, but based on how scared she looked, it wasn't good."

Before they could talk any more, Ty spotted a shadowed figure near a boat on the other end of the dock.

Normally, a person wouldn't draw his attention. But something about the way this guy moved seemed suspicious.

Ty's muscles bristled. "Excuse me!"

At his words, the man straightened.

He then jumped on a boat, reached into a compartment, and withdrew . . . a gun.

CHAPTER
ELEVEN

CASSIDY SAW the man pick up the gun.

Then she heard the bullets begin to fly.

"Get down!" she yelled.

They all dove behind the fish-cleaning station near them, ducking low to the ground.

The boat's engine fired to life, and the man began to zoom away.

As more shots rang out, Cassidy pulled out her phone.

She needed to call the marine police and the Coast Guard. There was no way Cassidy could catch up to this guy in time. Even if she had a boat at her disposal, it would take too long to get it moving.

She ended her call and then asked Ty, "Are you okay?"

"I'm fine." He nodded before rising to his feet and jogging back onto the dock.

Cassidy made sure Jimmy James and Kenzie were also unharmed before she followed Ty.

By the time they reached the end, she could already see the boat was too far away—too far to make out any identification numbers. Plus, it was too dark.

She let out a long breath as she watched the skiff disappear. "What was that about?"

"My guess?" Ty's steely gaze remained on the boat. "It's the same guy who shot at you earlier."

"I don't like the sound of that." Cassidy's muscles were growing tighter by the moment. "What is going on here in Lantern Beach? Do you think this has anything to do with Jasmine?"

"That's a good question."

Jimmy James and Kenzie joined them, both appearing shaken as they wiped gravel from their knees and elbows. Kenzie ran a hand through her long dark hair. But otherwise they seemed okay.

"That was unexpected." Kenzie shuddered, and Jimmy James wrapped an arm around her.

"Yes, it was," Cassidy agreed.

"I wonder if that was one of the same guys who came here a couple of nights ago," Jimmy James said.

"Tell me about these guys." Cassidy turned toward him, suddenly curious.

Jimmy James shrugged. "There were probably four of them. Like I said, they showed up two days ago in a cabin cruiser. Never seen the boat before—I would remember. It was a Grand Banks East Bay. Nice boat."

She took a mental note of the boat type. "Did you notice anything about them while they were docked here?"

"They were really quiet and kept to themselves. Didn't talk to anyone else. But they all left earlier today in that same boat."

Ty and Cassidy exchanged a glance.

"Did you overhear anything they were saying?" Cassidy asked. "See them do anything strange?"

"I didn't." Jimmy James glanced at Kenzie. "How about you?"

"Not really." Kenzie shrugged. "They kept to themselves."

"What about the woman staying on the boat with you?" Cassidy continued to press, determined to find answers. "Did Mary see them?"

"As a matter of fact, she did," Jimmy James said. "She freaked out and didn't leave the boat for probably twenty-four hours. Not until she knew they were gone. I asked if she knew them. She said no but that they looked like trouble. I couldn't disagree. They were some scary-looking dudes."

A clearer picture formed in Cassidy's mind.

But two questions remained: Where was Jasmine now? And how had that blood gotten on the doorframe?

————

While Ty and Cassidy waited for an update from the Coast Guard, Jimmy James agreed they could check out Jasmine's cabin.

Maybe they could find some answers there. Ty prayed that would be the case. They definitely needed a break.

Jimmy James led them to a lower deck and to a small room—one suited for staff instead of guests. Several articles of clothing were there as well as some toiletries and makeup.

But nothing of substance.

"Is this the only room Mary used while onboard?" Cassidy called over her shoulder to Kenzie, who stood alongside her in the small, confined space of the crew's quarters as Cassidy searched the room.

Ty and Jimmy James stood just outside in the

hallway—they all wouldn't fit inside the cabin at the same time.

"Mostly. There's a staff kitchen." Kenzie pointed to a room in the distance. "We told her she could keep some food in there, but that we didn't really want her to cook for safety reasons. She seemed okay with that."

"How did she pay?" Ty asked before trading places with Cassidy. Once in the cabin, he searched beneath the mattresses and in the drawers, acting as a second set of eyes.

"With cash." Kenzie shrugged as if she knew how suspicious that sounded. "I tried to talk to Mary several times, but she didn't seem interested in my help. I figured it was better to give her some privacy."

"Did she say how long she was going to stay?" Ty continued, still searching the room.

"We're supposed to have a charter in three days," Jimmy James said. "We told her she'd have to find somewhere else to stay when that happened. Honestly, I felt bad for her. I even thought about offering up my cottage to her while we're out to sea. But we didn't get that far."

"Did you see her with anyone?" Cassidy's gaze traveled back and forth from Jimmy James to Kenzie. "Hear her talking to someone?"

"No, she was alone the whole time," Kenzie said. "I didn't hear a peep out of her. Didn't even hear her talking on her cell phone."

Ty hadn't found anything of significance in the room.

There was nothing there that gave them any information.

He pictured Jasmine just grabbing her go-bag and running from her place in Canada. Then driving furiously. Using her fake passport to cross the border. Coming straight to Lantern Beach.

He was honored Jasmine had trusted him so much. But that trust was making things awkward now.

If Ty was single, this entire scenario would have been different. But now his loyalty was to Cassidy. Yet, at the same time, he couldn't turn his back on Jasmine either.

Cassidy's phone rang, and she glanced at the screen. "It's the Coast Guard. I need to take this."

She excused herself and paced up the stairs toward the salon.

Maybe she'd get more answers.

But all Ty had was more questions.

CHAPTER
TWELVE

BY THE TIME Ty and Cassidy made it to Blackout, Faith was already asleep. They kissed her, told his parents good night, and then went downstairs to talk to Colton.

Normally, Ty had these talks with him alone. But given everything that had happened on the island, Ty thought it was a good idea to include Cassidy.

The Coast Guard didn't have any updates for them so far. They were still searching. But it was getting late, and they hadn't found the boat yet.

Ty's gut feeling was that this guy was long gone.

Cassidy had done all she could do tonight. He saw the worry in her gaze and wished he could take that away. Unfortunately, he couldn't.

But, in the morning, Ty knew she'd start fresh.

Maybe tomorrow she'd find more answers.

They slipped into Colton's office. After sitting in the leather chairs in front of his desk, they gave him the update.

"Sounds like a rough day." Colton ran a hand over his face, appearing as if he'd also had a day. "Any idea where Jasmine might be right now?"

Ty shook his head. "No idea. But we need to find her. She needs protection. We need everyone here at headquarters to be on guard as well—at least until we have a better idea about what's going on."

Colton shifted in his seat and narrowed his eyes. "You really think Ravi's men could be on the island?"

"I do," Ty said. "Ravi has been obsessed with Jasmine ever since she disappeared. He saw losing her as a sign of weakness—and he believes others perceive him that way as well. He has an image to protect. He'll do anything to get her back. When he does, he'll make an example out of her."

"Why come after Jasmine after all these years?"

Ty had a couple of theories—but one he couldn't speak of. Only he and Jasmine knew about those details. As of now, no one else needed to know.

Instead, he said, "Ravi is a very proud man. Jasmine leaving him was the ultimate humiliation—something he'll never forget and never forgive her for."

Colton frowned and slowly shook his head. "Just

because you're not a Navy SEAL anymore doesn't mean that trouble stops following you, does it?"

"You can say that again," Cassidy muttered.

Ty slid a piece of paper across the table to Colton. "Before I forget, here's the contact information for Rex Houghton. He wants to hire us. He tracked me down personally, but I'm not sure how I feel about that."

Colton glanced at the guy's name. "I'll take over from here and look into this guy. You have enough on your plate right now."

Ty stood and took Cassidy's hand. "Thank you."

"Be safe, you two."

Ty heard the worry in his friend's voice.

Colton knew they were traversing in deep water too, didn't he?

Just how deep was too deep?

————

Cassidy's head pounded as she left Colton's office.

She'd been putting in some long shifts lately. For a peaceful little island, too much trouble found them. Mac and the town council had just approved for her to hire more officers. She needed to do that now before her entire team was overworked.

Ty tugged on her arm and pulled her to a stop in

the hallway outside Colton's office. He leaned toward her, his eyes narrowed with concern . . . but also love. "You doing okay? You look tired."

"I *am* tired. I feel like we can't catch a break."

He rubbed her arms soothingly. "I know. It's been a lot. When this mess with Jasmine is cleared up, I think the two of us should get away."

She raised her eyebrows, unsure if she'd heard him correctly. "Get away?"

"We can go somewhere warm. Somewhere cold. Somewhere. *Anywhere.* I don't care where."

"And Faith?"

"We can bring her with us." He circled his arms around Cassidy's waist. "Although, it would be nice for just the two of us to get away also. We've both had so much going on."

"We have." Cassidy rested her hands on Ty's chest, wishing she could melt into this moment. "Some downtime does sound nice."

"It does, doesn't it?"

"Are we ever truly going to find a good time?" She didn't want to ask and ruin the moment. But her question was valid. They'd both been so busy lately. Life seemed to be ruling them instead of vice versa.

"We won't find it—we'll make it. We need to get something scheduled. As soon as Brandon's wedding is over and this next session of Hope House is done, we'll go. Okay?"

A small smile tugged on her lips at the thought of his suggestion. "Okay. That sounds nice."

Ty grinned. "Perfect."

He leaned toward her and planted a long, slow kiss on her lips.

Cassidy melted at his touch.

If only she could forget about her problems for a while . . . but that seemed impossible.

The footsteps she heard thundering toward them only confirmed that.

CHAPTER
THIRTEEN

TY TENSED as he turned toward the sound.

Colton appeared in the doorway, adrenaline radiating from him as he paused.

"What's going on?" Ty rushed.

"Brandon's on duty tonight. He just found a body just outside our fence."

Ty's muscles stiffened as he stepped away from Cassidy. "A body?"

"He didn't recognize the man."

Relief swept through him. At least, it wasn't one of his guys. But Ty didn't want anyone to be hurt either.

Cassidy was already heading toward the exterior door, radio to her lips.

"Cassidy, wait," Colton called as he caught up with her.

He paused as if needing to drive home a point. After a moment of hesitation, Cassidy paused also.

"This guy . . ." Colton shook his head as if he didn't want to finish his statement. "It doesn't look good."

"What aren't you telling me, Colton?" Cassidy stared at him and tried to read his expression.

Colton swallowed hard. His gaze slid over to meet Ty's before moving back to Cassidy. "This guy . . . he had a gunshot wound in his shoulder."

Cassidy's eyes widened. "So it's most likely the man who was inside the house earlier? The one who tried to kill me?"

Colton frowned, and Ty knew that there was still more that his friend wasn't saying.

"There's a lot of blood," Colton continued.

"I understand." Cassidy took a step back toward the door, her gaze remaining on Colton. "Anything else?"

Ty waited for Colton to finish.

But he had a feeling he knew what Colton was going to say.

"He was beheaded." Colton's words sent a chill through the room.

And through Ty.

———

John the Baptist treatment, Cassidy mused.

Only someone who was sick and twisted would do something like this and call it that.

She stood outside the fence surrounding Blackout and stared at the dead man.

They'd already set up portable lights. All her officers were on the scene. Officer Bradshaw had brought his police dog and was now searching the area to see if he could pick up on any scents.

Their dead man was definitely the same guy she'd seen in their house earlier.

The same guy she'd shot in the shoulder. Possibly the same one who'd taken off in the boat earlier.

Had his colleagues decided that since he'd failed and was almost caught that he had to be punished? Had they then decided to make an example of him?

Cassidy hated to do it. She wanted to handle this herself.

But she knew this murder was bigger than her island police department.

She had put in a call to the State Bureau of Investigation. There was an agent for this area stationed in Raleigh. And he was on his way.

Until he arrived, she would need to preserve the scene. At this point it wouldn't surprise her either if the FBI ended up being called in. She also knew that Ty's captain was sending someone here.

Entirely too many people from the government were descending upon this island for her comfort.

She wanted to put a body sheet over the corpse so people didn't have to see it. But she couldn't risk contaminating it.

Maybe *she* was the one who didn't want to see it.

The scene was so gruesome that she almost wanted to throw up—and she'd seen a lot of gruesome scenes before. This one topped them all.

Ty appeared beside her and leaned close, lowering his voice. "You okay?"

She nodded and swallowed back her nausea. "I guess."

It wasn't a mistake that this body had been left here. Someone had wanted to send a message.

It had worked.

This scene . . . it was horrifying.

That was exactly the emotion someone had intended to evoke.

CHAPTER
FOURTEEN

BRIGHT AND EARLY THE next morning, Mac called Cassidy with an update.

More fish had washed up near the lighthouse. *A lot* more. *Hundreds* more.

People in town were noticing and becoming worried.

Cassidy promised to head right to the scene.

She ended the call and sucked in a deep breath as she readied herself to go. It had been a late night—a really late night.

By the time the NCBI had arrived, it was past midnight. Cassidy had stayed at the scene until they cleared it, which wasn't until close to four a.m.

The state was officially taking over the investigation into the man's death.

They didn't directly tell her that the man might

have ties to an overseas terrorist organization. They didn't have to.

Cassidy already knew.

The FBI had also been called, and they'd be here this morning sometime.

For now, Cassidy had other matters to attend to. Maybe the NCBI and FBI being here would be a good thing. Maybe they had resources to find answers that she didn't. She wasn't territorial.

She only wanted some progress in this case and safety for this little island town.

Before leaving Blackout, Cassidy lifted Faith into her arms and held her a few minutes.

Her little girl was already growing up too fast. Cassidy would never get these days with her daughter back. Somehow, she had to figure out a way to spend more time at home. Yet she also needed to keep this island and its residents—including Faith —safe.

The pull between the two responsibilities tugged at her. They were both the same and opposing. The same because her family was on this island. Different because her time was split between her work and her home.

The working mom gig wasn't always easy.

Hopefully, hiring more officers would eventually help ease some of her workload.

She kissed the top of her daughter's head before handing her back to Grammy. As they started to say goodbye, Ty strode into the apartment.

Kujo wagged his tail as he walked over to Ty and received a quick head rub.

Then Ty paused near Cassidy. "You taking off?"

"I am. More fish have washed up."

Ty's parents moved into the other room to give them a moment of privacy. Kujo followed.

He frowned. "Sorry to hear that. Be careful out there, okay?"

"I will be."

"You got in so late . . . I know you didn't get much sleep last night. Even then you were tossing and turning."

She cast him a glance. "And you didn't sleep at all. You were at the desk doing something."

He shrugged as if it weren't a big deal. "Researching."

"That's what I figured. You be careful too today, and let me know if you hear anything."

"Will do." Ty leaned forward to kiss Cassidy's forehead.

Why did the new life Cassidy had built here on this island feel unsteady, as if it were on the verge of breaking apart and shattering?

She wasn't sure.

But she hoped her gut feeling was wrong.

———

Ty ended his phone call and leaned back in his office chair at the Blackout Headquarters.

He'd checked in with a few of his military contacts.

They'd confirmed Ravi was still in Sahili. And he was still as vicious as ever.

Rumor was that the man was plotting something —though no one knew specifically what.

Could Ravi have discovered Jasmine's location? Followed her? Could he be sending his men to the US to find Jasmine and to exact revenge on the man who'd taken Jasmine away to safety?

Ty wasn't sure.

However, he did worry that, if he found her, he wouldn't be able to protect her.

Bringing her to Blackout would make the most sense, but the confines of this compound wouldn't be enough to protect her. His Blackout operatives could ward off gunmen. He had no doubt about that.

But Ravi was unconventional. What if he tried to attack by air? By sea? If he used weapons Ty and his men would be powerless to fight?

He thought about the nuclear program Jasmine

had helped shut down. What if there was an update on that situation in the ten years since Ty had been involved?

Or maybe it wasn't a nuclear bomb . . . what if it was a dirty bomb?

His jaw tightened.

He didn't like any of those options.

Ravi wasn't the type who'd simply send men in to shoot his enemies. He liked more grandiose displays of violence. Something that would show off his wealth and power.

Someone knocked at Ty's door, and he called for them to come in.

A man he'd never seen before stepped inside. The thirtysomething was fairly tall with short, dark hair.

He flashed his FBI badge.

Go figure.

Ty knew the feds would want to talk to him.

What he wasn't sure about was how much he could say. He'd called Captain Donaldson this morning, and the captain had told Ty to remain quiet, had reminded him about the security clearance required for anyone to know details.

So Ty would remain quiet for now.

"Agent Chen," the man introduced himself, his words clipped and no nonsense. "Do you have a few minutes?"

"Of course." Ty nodded to a chair. "Sit down."

He stiffly lowered himself into the seat across from Ty's desk.

"How can I help you?" Ty started.

"My team and I are questioning everyone at this facility to see what we can find out about the dead body that was found outside last night." Chen shifted stiffly, not a hint of personality in either his words or mannerisms. "Am I understanding correctly that you're a former Navy SEAL?"

"That's correct. Most of the men who work here are."

"Had you ever seen this man before? I'm assuming you got a look at his face last night."

"What was left of it." Ty instantly regretted his words and shook his head. "I've never seen him before, but I assume you'll talk with the police chief about it. Full disclosure—she's my wife. She can give you more information."

"I plan on doing just that."

"I'm assuming Colton has already gone through our security footage with you."

"He has." Chen nodded briefly and without fanfare. "He's been very helpful."

Ty stood, knowing his time was running out. "Whatever we can do to help you find answers, just let us know."

Chen stared at him another moment, and Ty fought to keep his expression neutral. "If you think of anything else that may help us, please let me know."

He slid a business card across his desk.

"I'll do that." Ty stared at the card but didn't touch it yet. "I don't want to cut this short, but I have another meeting to get to. Colton can get in contact with me if you need anything else."

"Thank you."

Ty waited for Chen to step out of the room before locking his office behind him.

He wanted to search the island. See if he could find Jasmine. Check in with Jimmy James.

Cassidy had probably already done some of those things. He'd touch base with her first so he didn't overstep.

Either way, he had to find answers, and there was no time to waste.

CHAPTER
FIFTEEN

CASSIDY SAW the crowd that had gathered around the fish kill and knew that this would be another interesting morning. At least fifty people were here.

She held up her badge as she pushed her way through before stopping on the edge of the group.

She did her best not to make a face.

Waste management had already cleaned up yesterday's fish. But it didn't matter. The putrid, decaying scent was even worse today.

Officer Dillinger stood between onlookers and the fish, trying to keep the crowd at bay.

"Is the water safe to go into?"

"What's causing these fish to die?"

"The waves are supposed to be killer today. Can I get into the water?"

"I came here all the way from New York! My vacation is a bust."

The questions flew from the people around her.

Cassidy turned toward them. "I assure you that we are looking into this and trying to take care of this in the most efficient manner. I do not recommend going into the water until we know that it's clear of any harmful bacteria or anything else that might have caused these fish to die."

"Are you sure that it's natural or could this be an environmental issue?" A woman stepped through the crowd, something about her demeanor striking Cassidy as different from the rest of the onlookers.

She looked casually professional, not like someone who was here on vacation.

"The government is investigating that also." Cassidy slid on her sunglasses, partly because of the brightness around her and partly to cover her annoyed expression. "But I'm not prepared to answer that question myself. I'm not, by any means, an expert in marine biology."

"I heard there's a new lab in town." The petite, Asian woman pushed her glasses up higher on her nose as she peered at Cassidy, a determined look in her eyes. "Does it have anything to do with this?"

Cassidy stared at the woman, caution stiffening her spine. She seemed more educated, her questions more pointed than the average person. "Are you a reporter?"

The woman made a face as if insulted. "A reporter? No. I'm Sierra Davis, the director of Paws and Furballs. We like to investigate any potential cases of animal cruelty, and I want to make sure this isn't what's happened here."

An animal rights activist, Cassidy mused. Just what they needed right now on top of everything else going on . . .

"It's like I said, we have the proper agencies looking at this unfortunate event. We have no reason to believe that the death of these fish isn't due to something other than an algae bloom or some other naturally occurring element. As I'm sure you know, fish kills do happen without the influence of humans."

"But they also occur with an overabundance of fertilizer and other runoff chemicals." The woman pushed her glasses up higher again. "Have you looked into those options yet?"

Cassidy narrowed her eyes, trying not to show her irritation. The woman was pushy—but her questions were valid. "Maybe the two of us could talk somewhere later. But right now, I don't have any more information to give you."

"I'll be around." Sierra appeared unaffected by

Cassidy's dismissal. "Is it okay if I take a closer look?" She nodded toward the fish as if she wanted to autopsy them on the scene.

"Feel free." Cassidy didn't see where the woman's examination would hurt anything.

As Sierra walked closer to the fish, Cassidy searched the crowd again. A woman standing at the back of the group caught her eye.

She wore a baseball cap and an oversized sweatshirt. Her dark hair was pulled back into a sloppy bun and sunglasses concealed her eyes.

But she still looked familiar.

Could that be Jasmine?

Cassidy couldn't be sure. Not from this distance.

But she needed to find out.

———

"I'm on my way," a deep voice said.

Ty flinched at the voice on the other end of his phone line.

He'd been outside walking to his car when his phone rang.

It was Captain Donaldson with an update.

"You're coming here yourself?" Ty paused beside a bench near the sidewalk to wait for his reply, relishing the comforting feel of the sunlight on his shoulders.

"That's right. I'm bringing two agents with me. You didn't tell anyone what was going on, did you?"

"No, I kept the details quiet. But someone was beheaded here last night."

"What?"

Ty explained the situation to him, ending with, "I have a feeling the FBI is suspicious."

Donaldson let out a grunt. "Stay quiet about it."

"You don't think it's important that the FBI knows what's happening right now?" It only seemed smart to keep them in the loop.

"You and I both know that this is beyond their level of clearance." A scolding tone filled his voice.

Ty found that interesting. Ravi clearly already knew that the US government had helped Jasmine escape. But what Ravi didn't know—or what he *shouldn't* know—was where she was located. But that might no longer be the case either.

There could also be things that Ty didn't know.

He remembered what Jasmine had told him. Remembered how she said she didn't trust someone within the government. That she thought someone was working for Ravi.

What if she was right?

Ty didn't want to think that was the case. But in

his years as a SEAL he'd seen all kinds of corruption. Most people could be bought for the right price.

He couldn't stop Donaldson from coming here. But he could be careful how he proceeded.

Ty drew in a deep breath before saying, "Call me when you get here, and I'll meet you."

Friend or enemy, he would keep Donaldson close.

"Will do," the captain said. "In the meantime, keep a lookout for the asset. It's of utmost importance that we find her."

Donaldson didn't have to tell him that twice.

CHAPTER
SIXTEEN

AS CASSIDY PUSHED through the crowd, they seemed to close in on her. Everyone had questions and concerns. They each wanted a moment of her time.

She couldn't blame them.

But they were going to have to take a number.

As Cassidy had already told them multiple times, she didn't have any answers yet. The first thing she'd do when she got to her office would be to make some follow-up calls about the situation.

For now, she left Officer Dillinger there to maintain orderly conduct.

There weren't that many places in this area where Jasmine could disappear. There were no buildings other than the lighthouse.

As Cassidy's gaze wandered toward the walkover

leading to the parking lot, she saw a woman disappear—but not before glancing back over her shoulder first.

That *was* Jasmine, wasn't it? She'd come out here to the beach today for some reason.

Now she was running.

Cassidy couldn't let this moment slip by.

"Hey! Wait!" Cassidy darted after the woman.

But it was too late. The woman had already scampered over the dune.

By the time Cassidy reached the parking area, a black sedan raced out of the lot and down the street.

Jasmine was gone.

Cassidy paused near the walkover and committed the license plate to memory. She'd run it when she got back to the office and see if that offered any answers.

She glanced behind her and considered walking back to the beach. But there was nothing more she could do there. Her best bet would be to go to the office and check in with everyone.

As she walked toward her SUV, she paused.

Another black-and-white feather rested on her door handle.

Seeing a feather once . . . she could dismiss that as a coincidence.

But twice?

No way.

This feather had been left on purpose.

The hair on her neck and arms rose.

She turned and scanned the area around her, hoping for a glimpse of what had caused this reaction.

She saw no one.

But she was nearly certain someone was watching her.

She couldn't stand out here and wait for this person to strike.

Instead, she climbed into her SUV. Her heart beat double time as she quickly locked the doors.

She needed to get back to the station.

Now.

————

At the station, Cassidy called Officers Bradshaw and Leggott into her office to debrief. Mac had also shown up—and right in time to join them.

"Okay, I need updates on everything that's been going on," she started as she sat behind the desk and took a sip of the awful police station coffee. "What do you guys know?"

Mac started. "The state took water samples from

several areas and is testing them. I expect them to have an update for us soon."

"That's good because we have a lot of people here who are very anxious about these dead fish." She frowned as she remembered the putrid scent of them. "Did you by chance talk to anybody at Ocean Essence?"

"I thought we should wait and see what the state says first."

"You're probably right." She glanced at Leggott and Bradshaw. "Either of you have any updates?"

Her officers shook their heads.

Mac studied her, clearly able to read her better than most people. "Do we have any idea what these men were doing on the island, Cassidy?"

Just as before, Cassidy desperately wished she could share more. That she could tell everyone in this room what was going on so they could be in the loop.

But she couldn't do that. Not yet.

"Something has clearly drawn these people to the island, and I'd like to get to the bottom of it," she said instead. "But I'm not there yet. In the meantime, we need to keep searching, to keep our eyes open for anything suspicious that might be going on."

"Yes, ma'am." Officer Bradshaw stood. "Anything else I can do?"

"We just need to make sure we try to keep things

calm on the island. I can already feel something stirring in the air, and I don't like it."

"I can feel it too." Officer Leggott narrowed his eyes as if he didn't like this situation any more than she did.

Her officers filed out of the room, but Mac stayed behind.

His discerning gaze fastened on Cassidy. "You want to tell me what's really going on?"

She frowned as she contemplated what to say. "I don't know for sure. But someone from Ty's past may be on the island. All the details are top secret right now—even from the feds."

Mac studied her another moment, and Cassidy knew he wanted more details. He was the mayor of this town. He took that responsibility very seriously.

He was also a friend and father figure.

"I promise, as soon as I can share more, I will." Her throat burned as she said the words. "Right now, I've been sworn to secrecy. It's a matter of national security."

"That sounds exactly like something I need to be looped in about." He raised his eyebrows, not bothering to hide his displeasure. "Especially if it puts people here on this island in danger."

"I couldn't agree more." Guilt nagged at her, but she pushed the emotion back. She had to rely on good sense right now, not emotion. "Let me talk to Ty. I agree that you need to know. I'll see what I can do."

Mac glanced at her another moment before nodding resolutely. "Okay then. I trust your judgment. But remember, there's a lot at stake here, and I'm in a position to help you figure this out."

CHAPTER
SEVENTEEN

TY KNOCKED at the door to Cassidy's office and heard her call for him to come in. Axel had taken him to pick up his truck since he'd left it at the house.

He stepped inside in time to see Cassidy staring at a computer with a frown on her face.

"Bad time?" He closed the door behind him.

Cassidy shook her head. "Not really. The FBI is setting up a command center in the conference room. They've already questioned me again, and I could use a break from their scrutiny."

"I bet."

She leaned forward, her eyes brightening just slightly. "Actually, I'm glad you stopped by because there are a few things that I need to tell you."

He lowered himself into the chair across from her

desk. He had a bag of food in hand from The Crazy Chefette. "I was hoping you might be hungry. I brought you one of those new rice and chicken bowls you like so much."

She took the paper bowl from him and opened the lid. The aroma of grilled chicken, cilantro, and garlic filled the air. "It smells delicious. Thank you."

"Of course." Ty pulled out his own bowl and stabbed a piece of grilled chicken before glancing back at Cassidy. "So, what's going on?"

"I think I saw Jasmine at the fish kill this morning. She was standing at the back of the crowd. By the time I got to her, she was gone." She scooped up some rice on her fork.

"That's too bad. I'm trying to figure out where she might be staying. But so far, no luck."

"I ran her plates. The car is registered to Regina Kudlow from Maryland."

"Regina Kudlow?" Ty rubbed his jaw. "I know Donaldson gave her a new identity up in Canada. Not sure about the Maryland plates. For all I know, Jasmine could have stolen the vehicle on the way down here."

"Is she the type to do something like that?"

"She's probably learned a lot during her years in hiding."

"I imagine she has." Cassidy reached into her desk drawer and pulled out the feather, which she'd placed in an evidence bag. She slid it across the table toward him. "Then there's this. Does it have any meaning to you?"

Ty didn't bother to hide his surprise. "Where did you get that?"

"One was left on my SUV yesterday, and I didn't think anything of it. But when I found another one today, I knew there had to be more to it."

"Ravi . . . feathers were his calling card." His voice sounded grim.

Her face went still. "Is that right?"

"He said it was some type of ritual his ancestors employed, so he wanted to keep it going. They'd leave a feather outside their enemy's property before an attack."

"So this is a war cry? A way of saying someone is coming for us?"

Ty frowned again. "Maybe."

"I don't like the sound of that." Her voice dropped to a whisper. "We need to loop Mac into this. He knows something's going on, and I can't keep him in the dark. It's not fair."

"I understand." Ty had wanted to keep this under wraps, but as the danger grew, he knew he couldn't continue to do so. They were going to need help to control this situation and keep people safe. "Captain Donaldson is coming with two of his men to look for Jasmine. He was supposed to be here already, but I just got a call. He's been delayed."

"Did he say why?" Cassidy stabbed another piece of chicken from her bowl.

"No, he didn't."

Instead of eating, she waved her plastic fork in the air as her gaze deepened with thought. "I'm surprised he's coming himself instead of letting his guys handle it."

"Jasmine is a valuable asset to this country. She risked her life to give us information we needed when we needed it."

"I'm not denying Jasmine did any of those things. My concern is the people here on this island." Cassidy pushed the rest of her food away and leaned back in her chair as if she'd lost her appetite.

She hadn't even eaten half her food.

Ty paused as he thought through their conversation. "I trust Mac. If you feel like you need to tell him, then tell him. The same goes for anyone else working for you. Just use discretion."

Cassidy's shoulders visibly softened as if she were relieved at his words. "Thanks. I appreciate that. So . . . what's new with you?"

"Unfortunately, nothing. I talked to the FBI this morning, but Donaldson instructed me not to tell them anything. Thankfully, Colton is handling things at Blackout. Meanwhile, every lead I've looked into appears to be a dead end."

"Just give it some time. You'll uncover something."

As Ty glanced at her desk, he squinted. He reached across it and pulled out a photo, partially hidden beneath one of her file folders.

"Where did you get this?" He stared at the picture of the boy.

"I found it at that rental house before I was nearly killed. Why?"

"This was the same rental house where those suspicious men were seen, right?" His voice sounded taut enough to pluck.

"That's right. But I had no reason to believe those men would have brought a picture like this with them. They didn't seem the type." Cassidy tilted her head as she studied his expression. "What's going on? Why are you so interested in that photo?"

"I'm not sure. I need to look into something first. Can I take it with me?" Ty's thoughts raced.

There was so much more he wanted to say. But not yet. Not until he knew more.

Cassidy's head tilted even farther. "Ty . . . ?"

He leaned toward her until their gazes locked. "I know what you're thinking. But I just need to do a little research first. Okay?"

She stared at him another moment before nodding. "Okay. Take the photo. But I want a full debrief as soon as your conscience lets you."

"You'll get that. I promise. Just give me a little time."

————

Ty was still keeping secrets from her, wasn't he?

Cassidy leaned back in her office chair after he left, and she rocked back and forth. The motion comforted Faith, and Cassidy had learned it soothed her as well.

Why would Ty keep more secrets? It didn't make any sense.

He wasn't private about his past—not with her.

But Cassidy knew the mission he'd been on with Jasmine was highly classified. She wanted to respect that. Still . . . why did she feel bothered?

She wasn't sure. She didn't like the chasm that seemed to be forming between them, however.

But she couldn't just sit here thinking any longer. She'd go crazy if she did.

Instead, she grabbed her keys and stood.

She wanted to talk to Jimmy James again and find out if Jasmine had returned to the boat last night. She had a feeling the answer was no, but she needed to double-check.

There was no room to be sloppy with this investigation.

She took Dillinger with her, but they both drove their own vehicles. They arrived at the marina a few minutes later and found a parking spot.

As they strode down the docks toward *Diamond of the Seas*, the scent of the sea rose around her—salty, yet somehow fresh. Seagulls squawked overhead as they begged for treats, and a fishing boat came in with today's haul—and the men onboard were downright jovial about their catches as they bragged about them on the docks.

They headed down the slip next to the yacht and spotted Jimmy James and Kenzie onboard *Diamond of the Seas*. They waved her in.

Dillinger agreed to remain outside and on guard while Cassidy talked to them.

After slipping off her shoes, Cassidy stepped into the main salon and saw that Jimmy James and Kenzie had been doing some paperwork. Bills and invoices and other things were strewn all over the table there, and soft music played in the background.

"Figured you'd show up before too long," Jimmy

James placed the stack of papers in his hands on a table beside him.

"Sorry to show up unannounced." Cassidy got right to the point. "Has Mary been back?"

"I haven't heard anything from her. I know that's not what you were hoping I'd say. I'm sorry I don't have anything else."

She hid her disappointment. "It's okay. I figured you'd call me if she showed up again."

"I did, however, find something when I was cleaning the boat up this morning." Kenzie stood to retrieve something from a table against the opposite wall.

She returned and handed Cassidy a yellow paper. The eight-by-twelve-inch sheet was mostly empty—except for ten digits scribbled in black ink at the center.

A phone number . . .

Cassidy studied it before looking back at Kenzie. "You think Mary left this behind?"

Kenzie didn't miss a beat as she nodded. "Jimmy James and I cleaned the boat thoroughly after our last charter. She's the only one who makes sense."

"Thank you. You mind if I take this with me?"

"Not at all."

Cassidy tucked it into her pocket and stepped toward the exit. "Thank you both for your help."

"Of course," Kenzie called. "I hope you're able to find her."

So did Cassidy.

CHAPTER
EIGHTEEN

TY STEPPED onto the beach to clear his head a moment.

Donaldson should be here soon, and Ty wanted to use that time to gather his thoughts. There was a lot going on—a lot of danger, a lot of decisions to be made, a lot of secrets.

He didn't like any of it.

Something about the ocean always made him feel better, made his thoughts clear.

He let the salty breeze wash over him. Listened to the birds singing overhead. Felt the power of the ocean as waves crashed on the shore.

His cottage stood behind him. He'd wondered if Jasmine might show up here again. If he might get some answers from her. If he might see for himself that she was still alive.

So far, she hadn't reappeared. He had no idea where she was or if she was even still on the island.

The moment brought back memories of when Ty had first approached her about escaping. Jasmine had known if she turned on Ravi, he would unleash a manhunt until she was found.

She'd outright rejected the idea.

Later, Ty had approached her a second time. This time, he could tell she'd been thinking about it. She asked for time. He'd promised a week, knowing from the rumors that Ravi was getting closer to making a deal to obtain nuclear material.

At the end of the next week, Jasmine had a bruise near her eye and she'd agreed to help.

Ty had wanted to rescue her right then. But she had to stay to get some information first.

Four days later, the red scarf had appeared.

Ty and Daniel had rescued her and whisked her off to safety and stayed with her for the first few days until another team arrived.

When Ty had to leave for another assignment, she'd broken down.

Ty had asked about her and learned she'd cried for the first month of being ripped away from her home country, friends, and family. In fact, she'd started several times to change her mind, to go back —even if it meant living in fear and danger.

But she hadn't gone back, despite the struggle.

Jasmine had been part of his assignment, so Ty couldn't allow himself to become personally invested in the woman. Still, the situation had been heart-wrenching on more than one level.

His thoughts continued to swirl.

First, he thought about those feathers . . . they were a war cry—as if the dead body outside the Blackout Headquarters hadn't been enough.

Then there was that photo . . .

He'd wanted to tell Cassidy everything. But the less she knew, the better. He'd been sworn to secrecy for the sake of national security concerning that nuclear bomb threat.

He'd vowed to never speak a word about her son.

Not even to the government. To his superiors.

Three months after her rescue, Ty had been given orders to temporarily help guard her. Jasmine had requested him.

When he'd arrived, Jasmine admitted that she'd hidden her pregnancy up to the seventh month. When she went into early labor, Ty had been there.

He'd helped her deliver the baby. Helped her care for her son.

He'd even set up the adoption through a private agency—and he hadn't told Donaldson about it.

Jasmine had made him promise to keep her son a

secret—and Ty understood the reasons why. Once her son was safely with a new family, Ty had been called to another assignment. He'd tried to forget about Jasmine and everything the woman was going through.

But how could Ty keep this information about Jasmine's son from his wife?

Unease jostled inside him.

He wasn't sure.

However, he was nearly certain the boy in that photo was . . . Jasmine's son.

No one was supposed to know she had been pregnant. No one could *especially* know that the baby was Ravi's. The dictator would stop at nothing to get his son back, to train him to fulfill a legacy of evil.

Jasmine had chosen to give her son up for adoption, claiming he'd be safer that way. Ty was inclined to agree. The kind of life Jasmine had to live wasn't suitable for a child.

Too much danger surrounded her. Going out was something she did only when necessary. She was practically living in a self-imposed prison.

Ty could only imagine that, even though she was away from Ravi, Jasmine now suffered in a different way.

His head pounded as memories pummeled him.

Jasmine had begged him to remain her bodyguard. But Ty couldn't do that. Not only had it not been his decision, but he'd seen she was becoming too connected with him.

There were professional boundaries that couldn't be crossed. But, for some reason, Jasmine said she only felt safe when Ty was with her—no one else.

She'd developed an unhealthy attachment to him, somewhat of a hero complex. For that reason, Ty had tried to put even more boundaries in place.

Jasmine hadn't seemed to notice. She'd been ripped away from everything she knew.

He could see that she was second-guessing her decisions. He'd reassured her she'd done the right thing. But he wasn't sure she was convinced.

He shifted, turning so the wind blew his hair from his face.

Where was Jasmine now? Where might she be hiding out on the island?

Had Ravi and his men truly found her? Were they on this island? Or, if they weren't on the island now, were they coming and going?

Ty had too many questions and not enough answers.

Above all, he had to keep his family safe. If Ravi found out he and Jasmine had a son . . . would he seek revenge by targeting Faith?

Ty's gut twisted at the thought.

He stared at the waves another moment. They were big today—powerful. A good reminder that life was so much bigger than just Ty. Than just Lantern Beach. Than just this time and place.

Ty scanned the beach one more time before taking a step back.

He'd cleared his head, and now he needed to get busy again.

But he'd only taken one step when someone pounced on him.

He hit the sand with a thud and turned in time to see a masked man on top of him.

Ty flipped the guy over, throwing the man off.

He was one of Ravi's men. Ty was certain of it.

The man was thin but wiry and strong.

He lunged at Ty again.

Then Ty saw something in the man's hand.

A knife glinted in the sunlight.

———

As Cassidy finished talking to Jimmy James and Kenzie, Dillinger got a call about a domestic dispute. He headed toward the scene, leaving Cassidy alone for only a few minutes.

She'd promised Ty she'd be careful, but she thought she'd be okay for just a while by herself.

As she headed from the marina toward her SUV, she spotted Sierra emerge from a marshy area behind the boat ramp and head toward her.

Cassidy's back muscles tightened. What was this woman doing here?

Cassidy didn't slow her steps, but she didn't have to. The woman joined her, easily keeping pace though she was a good seven inches shorter than Cassidy.

"Any updates?" Sierra placed a plastic tube into the black bag she held.

Cassidy waited for a seagull to stop screeching overhead before she answered. "Not yet. But state officials are here. We hope to hear their determination soon."

"Are you sure this doesn't have anything to do with the new laboratory that opened on the island?"

Cassidy paused and turned toward the woman, curious about her words and what she might know. "Is there something you're not telling me?"

Sierra crossed her arms, tucking her bag beneath one. "I just think it's strange that they opened this lab here on an island that's so isolated. It makes me wonder if Ocean Essence is trying to hide something."

Cassidy was careful to keep her expression

neutral. She didn't want this woman to see that she'd shared those same thoughts.

"We haven't found that they've done anything illegal," Cassidy said.

The words were true. Cassidy had been keeping an eye on them.

Sierra's eyes narrowed. "I decided to collect the water samples from around the laboratory today."

Cassidy sucked in a breath. So *that's* what she'd been doing. "Is that right?"

"I wanted to see how they compare to the water on other parts of the island."

"And were they the same?"

She pushed her glasses up on her nose. "No. As a matter of fact, there is a higher-than-normal concentration of sodium laureth sulphate in the water near the lab."

"What exactly is that?" Cassidy wasn't going to pretend to know.

"It's a chemical used in toothpastes, floor cleaners, and food thickeners. Sounds safe, right? But people need protective gear to handle it."

That didn't sound good. "I don't suppose it's naturally found in waterways?"

"Absolutely not. In fact, it's toxic to sea life." A frown flickered at the edge of her lips.

Cassidy's heart sped. She didn't like the sound of that. "And you're sure it's in the water near the lab?"

"Positive. I have six different test samples to prove it." She nodded confidentially, making it clear she didn't doubt herself in the least.

Cassidy crossed her arms, wanting to approach this subject carefully. "So you're saying this lab is using chemicals and letting them run off into our waterways? Because that's a serious accusation that could get them shut down."

"Look." Sierra stepped closer, her gaze narrowing. "Clearly, my goal is to take care of voiceless, helpless animals. But I also care about humans. Chemicals that leak into waterways have an effect on all of us, not just the fish and the birds. I hope that you're also concerned."

The way the woman had said the words was almost insulting. Cassidy didn't bother to hide her scowl. "My goal is to look out for the people here on this island, and I usually do that by trying to keep them safe from crime. This isn't truly my area, although I *am* keeping an eye on the situation."

Cassidy started to walk away again when Sierra caught up with her.

"Listen, I can tell you care about the people here," Sierra rushed. "That's why when I arrived in Lantern

Beach, I came to talk to you. I don't know who else to go to."

Cassidy paused again. "I know you came all the way out here to dive into this. I do appreciate it. I'll pass this information along to the state. If you hear anything else, I'd appreciate you sharing it with me."

"Of course." She pushed up her glasses again.

Cassidy stepped closer and lowered her voice. "And be careful. There are people on this island who don't like to be messed with. I don't want to see you get caught up in something dangerous."

Sierra didn't flinch, her expression making it clear she was always up for a fight. "Good to know."

"If I hear anything I'm able to share, I will let you know. How does that sound?"

"I appreciate it. I'm a working mom too, you know."

Cassidy raised her chin. "How did you know I was a mom?"

Sierra pointed to her shoulder. "You have just a little bit of drool there."

Cassidy followed her gaze and saw that she did indeed have some drool on her shirt. She rubbed it off—mostly. "Yes, I do have a daughter. She's teething."

"I have two kids. I want to leave this world a little

better place for them instead of worse. I'm sure you understand that."

Cassidy felt herself softening some toward the woman. Just yesterday, Cassidy had had those same thoughts.

Because of motherhood, she felt a moment of bonding with the woman. "Yes, I do understand that. Believe me, I'm doing everything I can."

"I'm glad to hear that. I'm glad you're in law enforcement also."

Cassidy narrowed her eyes. "What do you mean?"

"I just mean that something about some of the board members for Ocean Essence makes me feel uneasy. I don't trust them. If anything shady is going on, then the police will need to be involved."

Cassidy let those words settle on her.

But before she could think about it too long, her phone rang.

It was Ty.

She hadn't expected to hear from him just yet since they'd talked a couple of hours ago.

She excused herself from the conversation and put the phone to her ear. "Everything okay?"

But before she could barely get those words out, Ty rushed, "Cassidy, I've been . . . stabbed . . . I need help . . . now."

CHAPTER
NINETEEN

TY KNELT IN THE SAND, clutching his side. When he lifted his hand, blood covered his fingers.

The guy had come out of nowhere.

He hadn't even tried to fight fair.

Instead, the man had pulled a knife and had struck Ty in the side.

"This is just a warning," the man had muttered.

The next instant, he'd taken off across the sand.

Ty had staggered to his feet and attempted to chase him.

But he couldn't.

No matter how hard he tried to remain on his feet, he'd collapsed to his knees.

All he could do was call Cassidy—and he'd barely had the strength to do that.

He knew she'd be right there. That she'd call in backup.

Right now, his head swam as he fought to stay coherent.

Using his hands, he put pressure on the wound, trying to stop the flow of blood.

That had been one of Ravi's men, hadn't it? It was the only thing that made sense.

This guy had tracked Ty down in order to send a message.

This man could have killed Ty, but he hadn't.

Why?

Why just give him a warning?

Everything blurred around him, and Ty's thoughts wouldn't focus.

Finally, he thought he saw an SUV in the distance. He thought he heard sirens.

A moment later, Cassidy swerved into the driveway and threw her SUV into Park. The next instant, she found him. Knelt on the sand beside him. Gripped his shoulders as her worried gaze met his.

"Ty . . . what happened?" She scanned him for injuries and cringed when she saw his bloody side. "An ambulance is coming. We'll get you taken care of."

"I don't know how I didn't hear this guy coming." Ty's voice was raspy.

Yet that tactic was typical for Ravi. The surprise attack was exactly what the man had intended.

Cassidy stripped off her sweater and pressed it into his wound. "Did you see the face of the guy who did this to you?"

He was losing a lot of blood. Too much. His head swirled.

Ty shook his head. "He had dark hair, a beard and mustache. He was probably three inches shorter than I am and thin but muscular."

"Did he say anything?" Cassidy rushed.

"He just said that . . . this was a . . . a warning."

Cassidy's eyes widened, and she started to reach for his face. She stopped herself and continued to press her sweater into his wound.

"I don't like this, Ty," she murmured.

"Neither do I."

Just then, paramedics pulled into the drive and rushed toward them. Cassidy took a step back to give them room.

Ty could feel himself beginning to fade. He fought it with everything in him. He couldn't succumb to unconsciousness.

But before he could finish the thought, everything went black.

A cry left Cassidy's lips as Ty's eyes closed.

"No!" She tried to get closer, but someone pulled her back.

Mac.

"Let the paramedics do their job." Mac kept a hand on her elbow as if he feared she might collapse.

Maybe she would.

When she looked down at her hands, she saw the blood staining them. Covering them. Dripping from them.

Ty's blood.

At once, Cassidy realized how close she'd been to losing him.

How close she *still* was. He wasn't out of the woods yet.

Paramedics put her husband on a gurney and carried him to the ambulance. Cassidy started to follow behind when Mac's grip on her arm tightened.

"I'll drive you," he offered.

She didn't argue. Even though she wanted to be with Ty, she knew the paramedics needed space to work.

Everything felt like a blur as Mac helped her into his truck, and they started down the road.

"What happened, Cassidy? Talk to me."

At once, the whole story poured out. Ty had told her that she could share. So she did.

Mac listened, saying very little and asking only a few questions.

"So let me get this straight," Mac said once she finished. "An evil and vicious dictator may have sent his men to Lantern Beach to find his estranged wife, who could be hiding out here. Ty once helped rescue this woman, and now Ty is probably a target himself?"

Cassidy nodded, an ache pounding at her temples. "That sounds about right."

He clicked his tongue. "I don't like the sound of any of this."

"Is he going to be okay, Mac?" Her voice broke as she asked the question.

He patted her shoulder. "Ty is going to be fine. The ambulance will get him over to the clinic. Doc will fix him up."

But what would happen if Ty couldn't be saved? What if Cassidy lost him?

The question wouldn't stop echoing in her head.

Finally, they pulled up to the clinic. Cassidy already spotted Doc Clemson's car out front. He was here and ready to help.

But all Cassidy could do was pray for a good outcome.

CHAPTER
TWENTY

CASSIDY HAD BEEN WAITING AN HOUR, but it felt like days.

She'd already called Ty's parents to give them the news about their son's injury. As expected, they were upset and wanted to rush to the hospital. Cassidy had asked if they could stay with Faith and promised to give them updates. They'd agreed.

Everyone had assured her that things were under control and that Ty would be fine.

Cassidy wanted to believe them. But that familiar fear of losing everything had begun to creep in again. She'd lost everything once. She knew it was possible to lose everything again.

But she wasn't sure her heart would survive if that happened.

Oh, Lord . . . please help Ty. Protect him. Protect this

island. Give me wisdom to know how to handle this. Show me how to find answers. I need You, Lord . . . desperately.

Mac sat on one side of her and Tali, his wife, on the other. Colton had also come. Cassidy knew if she said the words her friends from her Bible study group would be here also. Braden, Lisa, Austin, Skye, Wes, and Paige had all become like family to her.

But she didn't want too many people here. Not yet.

Finally, Doc Clemson stepped out. The man was nearing seventy and had pale skin and thin, reddish-brown hair. He was a good man, and one of Mac's best friends.

His gaze found Cassidy's. "I got Ty stitched up. He's going to be fine. But he did lose a lot of blood. He's going to need a blood transfusion before we move him."

At his words, images of Ravi filled Cassidy's mind. She remembered the conversation she'd had with Ty, the one where he'd said Ravi liked to bleed out his victims before beheading them.

That fear became all too real for her.

She was the police chief. She wasn't supposed to be afraid. But when it came to protecting the people in her family, how could she not feel some anxiety?

Very few things were certain in this life. Though Cassidy knew she'd sacrifice herself to save those she loved, that still didn't mean she could promise anyone today or tomorrow.

"Can I see him?" She jumped to her feet, her voice cracking as she asked the question.

Doc Clemson nodded. "Yes. But I recommend sending him to a hospital over in Raleigh for observation."

Cassidy's stomach dropped all over again. "Is he that badly injured?"

"It's just a precaution."

"We'll have a doctor visit Blackout. We'll even hire a full-time nurse if we need to." Colton rose. "I'd feel much better knowing that he was under our watch instead of in a hospital."

Doc Clemson nodded. "If that's what you want to do, then that's fine. I'll do whatever I can to help arrange that."

Colton nodded. "Thank you."

Cassidy wiped her hands—which she'd washed when she arrived at the clinic to clean them of Ty's blood—on her pants. A moment later, she stepped toward his room, wishing she didn't feel the quiver of nerves she couldn't shake.

She stared at Ty as he lay in the hospital bed, his skin pale and his hair tousled. An IV had been inserted into the back of his hand, and numerous machines beeped in the background.

But he was okay. He was really okay.

A wave of relief swept over her at the visual confirmation.

Ty offered a faint smile when he saw her. "Hey there."

"Hey. You gave us a good scare." A sob caught in her throat as she paused by his bed and took his free hand into her own.

She'd told herself she would be strong, but now she could feel her resolve crumbling.

"I gave me a good scare too." Ty's voice sounded hoarse. "I'm usually much more on guard than this."

"The sand and the wind can mask a lot of sounds." Cassidy had been in similar circumstances.

It didn't matter how well-trained people were or how on guard. Sometimes, they didn't have the upper hand in the situation. It was just a reality of life.

"Colton wants to transfer you to the Blackout Headquarters for the rest of your recovery—after your blood transfusion," she told him, trying to stick to the facts instead of diving into her emotions. "Doc Clemson said you lost quite a bit."

Ty shifted, squinting as he did so as if fighting off pain. "That's probably a good idea. But I'm still not sure I like having you and Faith and my parents here on the island at all."

"I can't imagine anywhere else where we'd be safer than at Blackout Headquarters. We could try to get away somewhere and assume that no one would find us. But you and I both know that the chances of that are unlikely."

He squeezed his eyes shut again before nodding. "You're probably right. I'll be back on my feet by tomorrow. I'll help keep an eye on things."

She squeezed his hand harder. "I just want you to feel better. I know you're not a fan of lying around all day, but you have to take it easy for as long as Doc tells you to."

"Donaldson was supposed to be here . . ." He glanced at the clock on the wall. "An hour ago."

"Colton said Donaldson wasn't there when he left headquarters to come here."

"Do you know where my phone is?"

She glanced around. "Probably with your things over there."

"Can you grab it?"

"Of course." She found it then handed it to him.

He quickly scanned it before frowning. "He canceled. Said he'd have to delay coming until tomorrow."

"Did he say why?"

"No. No reason. But I find that odd."

Cassidy crossed her arms. "So do I."

"We've got to find Jasmine . . ." Ty's gaze locked with hers. "She's who they really want. She has the answers we need."

Cassidy nodded in agreement.

But they would have to worry about that later.

Right now, all Cassidy cared about was making sure Ty was okay.

———

Ty didn't want everyone to make a big fuss about him, but that was exactly what they were doing.

Colton and Doc Clemson had arranged a medical transport to the Blackout Headquarters. But it wasn't just a transport. It was a convoy—four guard cars flanked the ambulance.

He wanted to think it was overkill.

But he knew that wasn't the case.

He had no idea what else Ravi and his men were planning. But they weren't done yet. He was sure of that.

Cassidy rode in the ambulance with him, holding his hand.

He was still sore, but the knife had missed any vital organs. That was the good news. But Ty knew that, realistically, he'd at least be down for the rest of the day. Maybe longer.

That thought burned him up inside.

Was that why the man had stabbed him and left? Had he wanted to put Ty out of commission so he could be miserable knowing he couldn't keep his family safe?

His hands fisted at the thought.

He should have known better. He'd known exactly who he was up against. But the guy had still caught him by surprise.

That wasn't okay.

They pulled into the Blackout Headquarters and stopped near a back entrance. A small clinical room had been set up in the building, usually used for minor injuries.

That was where Ty would stay tonight.

As Ty was wheeled inside, he spotted his mom waiting near the clinic for him, worry clearly written in the lines across her face and in the tears in her eyes.

"I'm fine," he called to her as the paramedics paused the gurney near her.

But it was clear by his mother's expression that she didn't believe him.

As to be expected.

"You better be fine." She sniffled as she walked along beside him, trying to squeeze in every word possible.

"I am."

But how long would that be true?

This is just a warning . . .

The man's words echoed in his ears.

Ty might be physically confined to a hospital bed for the next several hours, but that didn't mean he couldn't plan out what needed to happen next in order to stop these guys.

There was no better time to start thinking about that than now.

———

The next few hours had been a whirlwind.

People had been in and out of Ty's room, and Cassidy tried to give them the space they needed. She knew it was important that his parents see him, but she hadn't let Faith go inside.

Even though the girl was too young to truly understand anything, Cassidy wanted to give Ty some time to recover before he saw Faith.

Instead, Cassidy had happily soaked in some time with her daughter. They'd played with blocks, read books, and had a snack.

But the whole time, Cassidy kept trying to replay what had happened. She couldn't stop thinking about Ty's attack, no matter how hard she tried.

Just as Cassidy put Faith to bed, Ty's parents returned. She didn't know what she and Ty would do without Grammy and Pawpaw. They were such a huge help, and they had a great attitude throughout all of it.

But Cassidy could still see that Ty's mom was upset.

As she stood with them in the living room, Cassidy pulled her mother-in-law into a quick hug. "Are you doing okay?"

"Kind of. It was one thing when these things happened overseas, and I didn't see Ty's wounds and injuries. But seeing him like this with my own eyes . . ." Del shook her head as she tried to hold herself together. Her voice sounded squeaky, and tears filled her eyes. "It's tough."

Cassidy squeezed her arm. The woman had truly become like a mother to her. She was everything Cassidy's own mom hadn't been—loving, kind, warm.

"I know it's tough," Cassidy murmured. "I'm going to find who did this."

Del's gaze locked with Cassidy's. "I need you to be careful. Clearly, these men are dangerous. Not many people can get to Ty the way this guy did. That worries me. It worries me for *your* safety also."

Cassidy didn't bother to argue with her. It wouldn't make Del feel any better.

Instead, she nodded. "My eyes are wide open. I promise. And I'll make sure to have someone with me watching my back."

"Good idea." She sniffled again.

Cassidy took a step away. "But right now, I'm going to go see Ty, okay?"

"You do that. Frank and I will be here for you, whatever you need." Del patted Cassidy's arm.

"Thank you."

Cassidy made her way downstairs to Ty's room. She stepped inside just as Colton left.

Ty was sitting up in bed, and the fire had returned to his gaze. Her shoulders loosened ever so slightly at the sight of him. His determination was a welcome change from the state she'd found him in earlier.

"I'm already tired of people making a fuss over me." Ty tilted his head to the side and narrowed his eyes as if annoyed.

Cassidy sat on the edge of his bed and took his hand. "Well, you're going to have to get used to it, at least until you're feeling better."

"I know it was a knife wound, and that knife wounds are serious. But I'm really okay. I promise."

His voice sounded convincing, but he had to

know some rest would be good for him—because of both the knife wound and the blood transfusion.

She squeezed his hand harder. "What if it had been me?"

Ty's face went pale. "Don't say that."

"Not so easy, is it? Listen, you gave us all a scare. So let us have our moment of worrying about you. You're so used to being the one who takes care of everyone else that you don't even know what to do with yourself."

A slight smile tugged at his lips. "I can't argue with that."

"No, you can't." Her grin faded as she stared at her husband and remembered the somberness of the situation. "I don't like any of this, Ty."

"I don't either. No matter which way I examine it, I can't figure out the best way to keep everyone safe."

"We'll get through this," she murmured.

Ty nodded slowly before grimacing again. "Yes, we will. I'm just afraid of what might happen in the meantime."

CHAPTER
TWENTY-ONE

CASSIDY FORCED herself to try to sleep—even though every part of her rebelled.

Still, she knew she'd be in a better mental state if she could rest.

She awoke early to shower and get ready. Faith was still sleeping, and Ty's parents were ready to take care of her, so Cassidy slipped downstairs to check on Ty.

He was already awake, and his color looked better this morning than last night. In fact, looking at him, she could hardly tell anything had happened. His eyes were bright, his motions sure.

"Good morning," she murmured, the huskiness in her voice surprising her. But she couldn't deny how emotional his knife attack had been for her—far more than she wanted to admit.

He offered a soft grin. "Morning. Good to see you."

She stepped closer, shutting the door behind her for privacy. "You been awake for long?"

He shrugged. "A couple hours. Dr. Mercer came by a few minutes ago to check on me."

Dr. Autumn Mercer had started working at the clinic with Doc Clemson a couple of years ago. Clemson was getting older and needed help, and Dr. Mercer fit the bill.

"What did she say?" Cassidy asked.

"That I'm looking good." Ty gave her a wink.

"Well, she's not wrong." A smile flashed across her face before quickly disappearing.

Cassidy sat on the edge of his bed and soaked in his features, searching for any signs that anything was amiss—that there was anything he wasn't telling her out of fear of making her worry. She saw nothing.

Still she asked, "You feeling okay?"

"A little sore, but overall I'm fine. No complaints."

She nodded at the cell phone he held in his hands and the notepad and pen lying in his lap. "I can see you're hard at work already."

His grin faded. "No time to waste, right?"

She couldn't argue with that. "Absolutely." Her

thoughts shifted. "Who was that boy in the photo, Ty? Can you tell me yet?"

A frown tugged at the edges of his lips. "I'm not positive, but I believe it's Jasmine's son."

Her eyes widened. "Jasmine had a son?"

He nodded somberly. "Yes, but Jasmine couldn't keep him—he wouldn't have been safe. Ravi isn't supposed to know about him."

"But that photo . . ." Her thoughts drifted into worst-case scenarios.

"I know. That's my concern also. It's just another reason to find Jasmine—so we can get more answers."

"I'm about to head out and see what I can find out. I'll check in with the FBI and see if they've discovered anything new—though I'm unsure if they'll tell me."

"Maybe they will."

"What about Donaldson?"

Ty pressed his lips together before answering. "I'm curious about this delay that prevented him from getting here yesterday. Last I heard, he's arriving this morning."

"Maybe he'll be able to tell you something."

"I hope so. We need to talk to Jasmine again." Ty's voice held a grim tone. "She's the key to resolving all this."

Cassidy studied her husband's face a moment. "You really think if we find Jasmine she'll have the answers?"

"I think there's a good chance that will be the case." Ty's jaw hardened as he said the words. "I feel like she knows more than she's letting on."

She nodded slowly and glanced out the window at the woods on the other side of the fence. A Blackout operative ran toward something in the distance.

Her back stiffened. Was something going on?

Ty saw the motion outside the window also, and his arms twitched as if he wanted to jump out of bed and check things out. Thankfully, he didn't.

"It's probably nothing," Cassidy murmured as she turned back to him, trying to soothe his apprehension. He needed to take it easy.

He said nothing, but his gaze kept skimming toward the window.

"I'll look for Jasmine," Cassidy continued, trying to distract him. "I just can't imagine where she is on the island right now. She's not staying on the boat or at the inn. I know she has a car, but we've scoured this island for it and haven't found it."

He finally pulled his gaze away from the window, but Cassidy didn't miss the frown tugging at the edges of his lips.

"There are only a few houses on the island that have garages," he said. "Maybe she's using one of them. It would be a good way to conceal her car."

"Good idea. I'll check those next."

He grabbed her hand and gave it a squeeze. "When you do, take someone with you."

Cassidy nodded, knowing she needed to get going. Her to-do list was a mile long—and people's safety depended on getting these things done. "I will."

Just then, a gunshot cracked the air.

Cassidy jumped to her feet. "What was that? Are there any training exercises going on today?"

Ty's jaw thumped. "I don't think so."

A bad feeling churned inside her. "I'll go find out."

Before she could leave the room, a shadow appeared in the doorway.

It was Rocco Foster, another one of Blackout's operatives.

"We have a problem." His British accent stretched through the room.

"What's going on?" Ty pushed himself up higher in his bed, a no-nonsense look in his gaze.

"We just spotted a drone flying over the building. Maddox shot it down. But someone is clearly trying to gather information on us."

Cassidy's gut twisted tighter.

The people behind these crimes weren't playing. They weren't slowing down either.

That meant she would need to speed up.

————

It was killing Ty not to be out there with the rest of the gang and able to hear an update on what had happened.

But sending up a drone sounded exactly like something Ravi would do.

He knew the way this guy operated.

Footage from the device would be a way to get a lay of the land. To count how many guards were stationed outside. To look for areas of vulnerabilities at their headquarters.

Even knowing that, Ty couldn't send everyone here at Blackout running. What kind of security agency would they be if they did that? It certainly wouldn't inspire confidence.

Only a few minutes after Cassidy left for work, someone knocked at the door. Ty looked up and saw Colton there.

"You have an update?" Ty rushed.

Colton stepped into the room, his expression tightly lined. "Finley is examining the drone right now to see what kind of footage was recorded." Finley, Brandon's fiancée, was the CEO of a tech company. "Most likely, the information it collected was transmitted to another server."

"In other words, whoever sent that drone up got the information they wanted."

Colton nodded, his gaze grim and humorless. "Yes. Until we shot it down, at least. I've already increased the number of people guarding headquarters. I've told them to not only search the outer perimeter but to also watch the skies and, of course, the water. We really just don't know what this guy is planning right now."

"Smart thinking. You're right. Until we know what might be happening, we need to be prepared for anything."

Colton took a step back toward the door. "I just wanted to give you that update. Part of me doesn't want to loop you in on this because I know you need to relax and recover. But I know you're not going to take it easy unless you know what's going on."

"Yes, please keep me in the loop. I need to know what's happening so I know how best to protect my family." Ty shifted, the IV in his arm tugging against his skin.

"Of course." Colton paused by the door. "Also, before all of this happened, I called Rex."

Ty had nearly forgotten about that guy in the midst of everything else. "And?"

"He's gotten some other threats. Right now, they're all via text—except for that bowl of fake blood. I was going to send Hunter out to offer protection. But now I'm wondering if we need to keep all hands on deck here at the headquarters."

Ty quickly did some mental calculations. "How many guys do we have here instead of on assignment?"

"Twelve. But some of them are rotating in and out at Ocean Essence."

At the mention of the company, his gut tightened.

Cassidy had qualms about the laboratory, and Ty understood why. Something about the company didn't sit right with him either.

"That's fine if Hunter and another operative want to switch off while guarding him—as long as Rex understands the terms of our contract."

Colton nodded. "I'll worry about that—as soon as we figure out this whole drone situation."

Ty's thoughts drifted back in time. A couple of years ago, an enemy had sent drones equipped with guns to the island. To say it hadn't been a pretty sight would be an understatement, but thankfully no one had been seriously injured. That was only because of the quick actions of some fellow Blackout operatives.

Ty wanted to know for certain if the drone was Ravi's. But he knew Ravi was too smart to leave any evidence that would point back to him.

Ty hoped Captain Donaldson would arrive soon and provide some answers instead of just more of a headache.

But that remained to be seen.

CHAPTER
TWENTY-TWO

CASSIDY FELT a new determination in her steps as she left Blackout Headquarters.

She kept her eyes wide open as she traveled down the road, watching out for any surprise ambushes. Though, by nature, a person couldn't anticipate them, she would try anyway.

She'd already called Officer Dillinger, and she'd pick him up to accompany her today. It was only smart.

She'd also called Mac and given him the update on the drone. He said they were still waiting on the water results from the state lab, but he'd been advised that they should go ahead and close the beaches where the dead fish washed up. Cassidy promised to put Leggott on it and then gave her officer a call with the instructions.

She made it to the station in record time, and Dillinger was outside waiting for her.

He climbed in with two cups of coffee and a brown paper bag. "Lisa dropped this off, along with breakfast sandwiches. She wants to make sure you're eating."

"She's sweet like that. Thank you."

Dillinger placed Cassidy's coffee—as well as his own—in the cup holder between them before slamming the door. The scent of bacon and eggs filled the SUV, and Cassidy's stomach grumbled. When she had the chance, she should try to eat.

As she started back down the road, Dillinger glanced at her. "How's Ty?"

"He's doing fine. The situation could've been much worse."

"I can't believe he was stabbed. No one ever surprises Ty." Dillinger rubbed a hand over his face.

"We're dealing with some pretty dangerous people." Cassidy could say that much. Anyone observing the situation could see the truth in her words. But she still couldn't share too many details, and it was killing her to keep everyone in the dark.

"This doesn't have anything to do with the fish kill, does it?" Dillinger glanced at her again.

She grabbed her coffee and took a sip to buy herself some time. The bitter yet aromatic flavor covered her taste buds. "I don't think so. But that situation concerns me also. I plan on looking into that later. Right now, I'm searching for a woman of interest."

"Who would that be?"

Cassidy considered what to say, knowing she needed to choose her words carefully. "She's someone Ty worked with on one of his past missions. We believe she found Ty here in Lantern Beach and that she's in danger."

"That would have been nice to know earlier." Dillinger twisted his neck as if trying to process her words.

"Unfortunately, it wasn't my information to share. In fact, I shouldn't have even told you that much. It's all classified." She gripped the wheel more tightly.

"I get that." Dillinger stared out the window. "So what are we doing now?"

"We're going to search the island looking for the black sedan I last saw this woman driving. We've already scoured Lantern Beach for the vehicle, but maybe she's staying at one of the few houses on this island with a garage. Otherwise, we would have seen her car."

Dillinger shrugged. "She could have left on a ferry."

"She could have, but I don't believe that's what

happened. The ferry crew is keeping an eye open for a car that matches her description. So far, there has been nothing."

Cassidy couldn't help but think there was more to Jasmine's story. Maybe even more than Ty knew.

She glanced at each street they passed as she headed to the south end of the island. She was all too familiar with the grid system she'd set up on this island for searches such as this. This wasn't her first rodeo, so to speak.

She knew where a majority of the homes with attached garages were located, but she needed to be absolutely certain and not miss anything. For that reason, she would search each street.

Most of the homes in this area were built high on stilts because of the floodwaters that came during big storms. Because of that, most homes didn't have a garage. If a house *did* have a garage, there were vents so water could flow through, and people didn't keep anything permanent inside.

Cassidy and Dillinger searched street after street, checking every house with a garage for any sign of this car. As she drove, she munched on the breakfast sandwich, grateful for her friend's thoughtfulness. Even though she didn't have an appetite, she needed to eat.

Thirty minutes later, Cassidy and Dillinger still

hadn't discovered anything. But she wasn't ready to give up yet. She needed to be certain.

They still had two miles to search.

"How's Lisa doing?" Cassidy knew the conversation seemed mundane considering everything going on, but she truly wanted to know. She hadn't really had a chance to sit down and chat with her friend in more than two weeks.

"Busy but good. Having Cadence here is a big help."

Cadence was Lisa's cousin, who was assisting her at both the restaurant and with Lisa and Braden's children.

"I can imagine," Cassidy murmured. "Hopefully, Lisa's ready for the summer rush."

"She's looking forward to it. Coming up with all kinds of new recipes—and, as you know, that's one of her favorite things."

Cassidy smiled. Her friend was skilled at creating unique food combinations. And people *loved* them. They came from all over just to try food from her restaurant.

"She mentioned bringing some food by for you and Ty. But with everything going on, she wasn't sure if that would be a help or hinderance."

"Tell her thank you. If we're able to take her up on that offer, I'll let her know."

A moment of silence passed.

"The man at the house, the one we shot before the place went up in flames . . ." Dillinger started. "Is he the guy who was . . . beheaded? Is he connected with all this?"

"I don't know for sure, but that's the working theory right now. I believe there are a small group of men traveling to and from the island via boat—and that they're connected to the woman I'm searching for. I believe they're also searching for this woman and have harmful intent. The Coast Guard is on the lookout for any suspicious activity out on the water, but so far there's been nothing."

"I see." Dillinger pointed to a house at the end of the lane they'd just pulled into. "There's another garage."

"Let's check it out."

Cassidy pulled to a stop in front of the house and put her SUV into Park. Then Dillinger got out and peered into the garage through the window near the top of the door.

She didn't have high expectations. So far, they'd had no luck.

But when she saw Dillinger's back muscles stiffen, she knew he'd found something.

He motioned to her, and she cut the engine. Then she pulled her gun as she approached the house.

Doc Clemson, who was officially the doctor in charge of Ty's care, had cleared Ty to get out of bed and move around some. But Ty had been given strict orders to stick to sedentary activities.

The IV had been removed from his arm, and he'd been able to take a shower and change into some fresh clothes.

Just as he stepped from his room, his phone buzzed.

It was Donaldson.

He and his men were finally on the way here, and they wanted to land their helicopter at the Blackout Headquarters. They'd be arriving in twenty minutes.

Ty cleared the impending landing with Colton.

As Ty waited for them to arrive, he sat across from Colton, Brandon, and Finley in the conference room. The dismantled drone lay scattered on the table between them. It had already been checked over to make sure no listening devices had been planted on it.

"Can somebody bring me up to speed on this?" Ty grimaced as pain radiated from his side. He didn't want to even hint at his discomfort, however. If he did, his guys would no doubt try to put him back on bed rest.

That wouldn't be happening.

Colton glanced at Finley.

"There are no identifying markers on the machine itself," Finley started. "However, this brand is top-of-the-line with amazing technology. Most likely, the person who purchased it was someone with access to a lot of money. The camera on it was transmitting everything back to the drone's pilot."

"Are you able to find out where they were operating from?" Ty felt a headache starting. He'd take more pain relievers as soon as this meeting was over.

She frowned. "I'm working on that, but it's unlikely."

That wasn't what Ty wanted to hear, though he wasn't surprised.

Ravi was smart, and if he was behind this, he would be sure to cover his tracks.

The man had all the resources he wanted at his disposal.

"Is there anything this camera may have picked up that we should be concerned about?" Ty glanced at Colton.

"Only the layout of our campus." Colton's serious voice made it clear that was concerning. "There were no training exercises going on and no one of particular interest here at the base when the device went over."

"We would have seen the drone if it had gone over the headquarters earlier, correct?" Ty tried to think through the scenario from every angle.

"Not necessarily. Drones can travel upwards of a hundred miles an hour and operate thousands of feet in the air. It's hard to spot them sometimes."

"Anything higher than four hundred feet risks in-air collisions with other aircraft," Ty noted. "Drone operators have to have FAA approval for anything above that, right?"

"That's correct," Colton said. "But these guys don't play by the rules. We're going to be implementing some new security protocols because of this."

"Smart thinking," Ty said. "Somebody may have wanted to get the layout of this place. But they also may just want to keep us on edge and make us think they have the upper hand."

"Can somebody tell me what's going on here?" Brandon shifted. "I feel like I'm in the dark about something."

Ty and Colton exchanged glances.

Finally, Ty spoke. "I wish we could tell you more, but as of right now it's on a need-to-know basis. Hopefully, I'll be cleared to give more details soon." He glanced at his watch. "Maybe in ten or fifteen minutes, for that matter. But for now, I have no choice but to remain tight-lipped."

"What's happening in ten or fifteen minutes?" Brandon asked.

"An old friend from the military is coming here to provide an update. I'm hoping to have some more answers then." But what were the chances Donaldson would be forthcoming with information?

Slim to none, if Ty had to guess.

CHAPTER
TWENTY-THREE

AS SHE WALKED toward the house, Cassidy knew she had to proceed with the utmost caution.

She joined Dillinger by the garage door and peered inside to confirm what he'd seen.

Sure enough, a dark sedan was parked there.

It looked exactly like the one Jasmine had driven.

Her breath hitched.

Though it was too dark in the garage to see the license plate, Cassidy would bet it matched the one she saw earlier.

She and Dillinger headed toward the front door, guns drawn.

When they reached it, she and Dillinger stood on each side. She tried the knob, but it was locked.

She still had a master code for all the homes this

particular rental agency took care of. She found the numbers in her phone and punched them in.

Quietly, she opened the door. Usually, she'd announce her presence. This time, she needed the element of surprise.

She and Dillinger stepped inside, and Cassidy cautiously walked along the first floor.

The place had a similar setup to the other house they'd searched—the one where the intruder had shot the fireplace.

The downstairs—all bedrooms—was clear.

Cassidy indicated for Dillinger to follow her upstairs.

Her back muscles tightened as she anticipated more trouble. She hoped that wouldn't be the case, but she prepared for it.

The open concept upstairs made it easy to do a quick scan of the place.

The living room and dining area appeared empty with nowhere for anyone to hide.

Cassidy's gaze stopped at a coffee mug on the kitchen counter.

She paused by the mug and placed the back of her hand against it.

The ceramic was still warm.

Her heart rate quickened.

Someone *had* just been here.

She glanced at Dillinger and nodded, silently letting him know to be careful.

The only other place to search on this floor was the master bedroom and bathroom.

The door leading into it was open.

Quietly, Cassidy stepped inside and glanced around the cheerful room, decorated with whites and teals.

At first glance, the room appeared empty.

But when she walked to the closet and opened the door, someone lunged at her.

————

Donaldson arrived at the Blackout Headquarters right on time.

Ty stood outside waiting for him, the wind from the helicopter blades whipping his hair around and making it unruly.

He felt weaker than he wanted to admit. But Doc Clemson had said that was normal. Ty could push through this and work on resting later.

Figuring out what danger lurked on this island was more important.

As soon as the blades stopped spinning, the helicopter operator hurried from the aircraft and opened another door.

Donaldson stepped out.

Even with his retirement not far in the future, the man still had a commanding presence, Ty noted as the man briskly walked toward him. He wore his uniform, every white hair was in place, and even his wrinkles somehow looked refined.

Ty saw two men in suits also climb out of the copter and trail the captain.

FBI? CIA? An agency working off the books?

It could be any of those scenarios.

The three men would be staying here on the Blackout campus—a decision Ty had some reservations about.

When Donaldson approached him, Ty offered a salute and stood at attention.

"At ease." The captain then nodded at Colton, who stood beside Ty. "Lead the way inside."

"Of course," Ty murmured, not surprised the man had instantly taken charge of the situation.

Donaldson remained all business as they stepped inside the Daniel Oliver Building and headed to Ty's office. Normally, they'd head to the conference room, but the drone was still there.

Ty hadn't decided yet if he would share that information with Donaldson. He would need to play it by ear.

Colton excused himself as they reached the door

to Ty's office. He already knew he couldn't be a part of this meeting.

Not yet, at least.

Ty didn't know the two men with Donaldson, and they didn't say much. He could only assume they were Donaldson's little soldiers, the guys who would do whatever he told them. They'd briefly muttered their names—Henrico and Byers.

As Ty, Donaldson, and Donaldson's men settled around his desk, Ty didn't have a chance to start with pleasantries.

Donaldson jumped in first, his voice demanding as if he were a strict father. "Any luck in locating the asset?"

Ty shook his head. "We've been searching all over the island, but we haven't been able to locate her."

A sudden pain in Ty's side caused him to touch the bandage over his wound. The burst of discomfort reminded Ty that he could have died. That he might not be here right now if the blade had twisted in the wrong direction.

That only made him feel a new sense of determination.

Donaldson's eyes narrowed as he studied Ty. "What did I miss?"

Ty went through the story about what had

happened yesterday, and Donaldson's gaze darkened with every new detail.

"It definitely sounds like The Executioner is here on the island." Donaldson bristled as he said the man's nickname.

"I thought you said you had an eye on him in Sahili?"

A frown flicked at Donaldson's lips. "We've lost track of him. Actually, the original intel we received may have been skewed. My men may have simply spotted someone who looked like Ravi instead of Ravi himself."

Ty's lungs tightened. He wasn't surprised. The man had probably planned it that way. He probably had doubles for occasions just like this.

Ravi was one person no one wanted to be here. For a man like him to go through all this trouble . . . he would only do so if he had nefarious reasons. Serious reasons.

Deadly reasons.

"We also shot down a drone over the Blackout Headquarters yesterday." Ty decided to share the information. Colton had said he could use his own discretion on the matter, and Ty didn't see where it would hurt anything for Donaldson to know. "We've been examining it and looking for evidence."

Donaldson bristled. "And you're just now mentioning this?"

"We have a lot of enemies," Ty explained. "We had to be certain the drone was connected with The Executioner and not someone else."

"And?" Donaldson tapped his finger impatiently.

"We're still uncertain. You and your men are welcome to take a look at the device."

"We'll be doing that."

Ty didn't appreciate the man's accusatory—or controlling—tone, but he brushed it off, knowing he had bigger battles to fight right now.

"Are there any updates as to how the asset's location was compromised?" Ty stared at Donaldson's face, searching for any signs of deceit.

He saw nothing of concern.

But the man was always stoic, so he could be hard to read.

"We're looking into several possibilities," Donaldson started. "But regardless, The Executioner has his people out there looking for the asset. That's what has happened every time we've had to relocate the asset. She's not on social media, but our gut instinct is that these men have been able to hack into various security camera servers and run a facial recognition app."

"That's pretty high-tech stuff," Ty said. "Plus, it

involves a huge time commitment to comb through all of that."

Donaldson offered an affirmative nod. "You're absolutely correct. You and I both know that Ravi is obsessive. He wasn't able to let it go that Jasmine got away."

Ty considered telling him about Jasmine's son. But Donaldson had no idea the boy existed. Ty wasn't sure he wanted to be the one to tell him.

It really needed to be Jasmine's call.

"So what now?" Ty leaned back in his leather chair. "You and your men are here. I assume you'll look for the asset and . . ."

"We're going to search every inch of this island. It's imperative that we find the asset before The Executioner does."

Something about the way he said the words struck Ty as odd. Maybe it was his tone. Ty wasn't sure.

What wasn't Donaldson telling him?

Clearly, the government had promised to keep Jasmine safe. That was exactly what Ty wanted to see. For Jasmine to be protected.

But the way Donaldson said the words made Ty wonder if there was more to this story.

What if Jasmine knew something about the US

government that Donaldson didn't want her to share?

The question lingered in his mind and wouldn't leave.

What else exactly was going on here?

CHAPTER
TWENTY-FOUR

CASSIDY BRACED herself to fight the assailant.

But instead of attacking, the intruder tried to dodge around Cassidy.

Cassidy blocked the way.

Then her vision focused.

Jasmine came into view.

Desperation filled the woman's gaze.

True desperation.

Jasmine was honestly terrified, Cassidy realized.

The woman clutched a kitchen knife. Strands of hair had escaped from her ponytail. She looked weary yet frantic at the same time.

"Calm down." Knowing Dillinger had her back, Cassidy holstered her gun and patted the air with her hands. "It's just me. Cassidy."

Jasmine stared at her a moment, an almost feral look in her gaze.

Cassidy remained braced, knowing Jasmine could still strike at any time. She was clearly scared out of her mind.

"We aren't here to hurt you," she murmured.

Dillinger kept his weapon in hand, and Cassidy cast him a quick glance.

He nodded, knowing to remain guarded.

Finally, Jasmine lowered her knife as realization seemed to fill her gaze.

"Cassidy?" Jasmine stared at her, her voice trembling. "I was so sure . . . I thought you were . . ."

She glanced at Dillinger and then pressed her lips closed, not daring to say Ravi's name in front of the stranger.

Cassidy stepped closer. "We've been looking for you, Jasmine. Ty and I have been worried. You disappeared, and we found the blood on our doorway. Naturally, we thought something had happened to you."

"I'm sorry to have caused trouble. But I second-guessed my decision to find Ty. I thought you would convince him not to help me, so I panicked and ran. When I did, I cut my arm on the side of the door. I didn't mean to leave a mess. But I had to keep moving, and I couldn't look back. It's the nature of life on the run. I've become somewhat of an expert over the past decade."

Cassidy couldn't argue with Jasmine's statement. Cassidy had been on the run herself, and she knew how desperate feelings led to desperate acts.

For that reason, she should feel entirely more compassion toward this woman. But she didn't, and she couldn't pinpoint why.

"Were you followed?" Jasmine's gaze darted behind Cassidy and Dillinger as if searching for danger, as if waiting for the other shoe to drop.

Cassidy shook her head. "After what happened to Ty, I was watching the whole time, and I even checked my vehicle for trackers. There was nothing."

Jasmine studied Cassidy, her eyes widening. "Something happened to Ty?"

Cassidy shouldn't care that this woman sounded so concerned about Ty. But part of her did. It seemed as if Jasmine had claimed certain rights to Ty, that she was almost territorial over him.

Resentment rose in Cassidy, but she pushed the emotion down and tried to remain professional. Ty didn't feel the same way about Jasmine, and that was what was important.

"Someone stabbed him." Cassidy kept her voice matter-of-fact, not daring to touch on her emotions.

Jasmine gasped, and her hand flew over her mouth. "Oh, no! Is he . . . dead?"

"No, he survived. But it could have been much worse."

Jasmine stepped away from Cassidy and began to pace. "He's here, isn't he? He tracked me down. He promised he would. I suspected he was in the States, that he'd found me. This seems to confirm it. What am I going to do?"

"You mean your ex-husband?"

Jasmine stared at her a moment before nodding hesitantly. "Yes, my ex-husband."

Cassidy observed the woman a moment. She didn't have long to decide how to handle this situation. She and Jasmine needed to get out of this house. It wasn't safe for them to be here.

She watched Jasmine pace. Saw the distress on her features. Heard the desperation in her voice.

Though she didn't quite trust Jasmine, she felt certain the woman truly feared for her life.

Plus, Ty wanted to help her.

Cassidy was going to trust her husband's judgment.

She turned to Jasmine, a decision solidifying in her mind. "I'm going to take you back to Blackout with me."

Her gaze widened. "To where? What is this Blackout place?"

"It's the only place you'll be safe." Cassidy had resisted the idea, but she would insist that a guard be placed with Jasmine the entire time—just in case the woman wasn't trustworthy. "Ty is there."

As if Cassidy had said the magic words, the woman relaxed. "In that case . . . let's go."

Cassidy stepped forward and held out her hand. "I'll take that knife now."

Jasmine looked at her hand as if she didn't realize the weapon was still there, then she handed it over and darted out of the room.

Cassidy and Dillinger filed out after her.

The longer they stayed, the more danger they would all be in.

―――――

As Donaldson and his men grabbed some coffee from the dining hall, under Colton's supervision, Ty's phone rang. He looked at the screen and saw it was Cassidy.

With one more glance at Donaldson, he stepped away and put the phone to his ear, careful to lower his voice so he wouldn't be overheard. "Hey. What's going on?"

"We found her," Cassidy announced.

His heart raced at her proclamation. "Jasmine?"

"Yes. I want to bring her back to Blackout. I don't know where else she'll be safe."

Ty glanced at Donaldson again, and his back muscles tightened. "If you bring her here, we're going to have to keep her out of sight for now."

"Why? What's happening?" Concern edged Cassidy's voice.

"Donaldson's here with two of his men. I'm not sure who we can trust. But I have a feeling that either Donaldson, one of his men, or maybe even a member of the FBI might have something to do with all this."

Cassidy let out a soft gasp. "What?"

"We can talk later. I can't say very much right now."

"Okay. So what should I do?"

"Have Jasmine hide in the back seat when you arrive. Come in the back entrance of the Oliver Building. I'll figure out a way to distract Donaldson, and then we'll get her into a secure room. I'll station a guard outside her door. And I'm not going to tell anyone where she is. You shouldn't either, okay?"

"Okay. But Dillinger is with me."

"We can trust Dillinger and the rest of our Blackout team. But no one else for now."

"I don't like the sound of that." Cassidy's voice dipped lower with concern.

"Believe me, I don't either." Ty's gaze lingered on Donaldson as he took a sip of his coffee and stared out the window at the Blackout campus.

Ty wanted to believe that his former leader could be trusted.

But nothing was certain right now.

Ty's parents and daughter were under the same roof as this guy.

Cassidy would be here soon.

And Jasmine.

Which meant the stakes couldn't be higher.

————

Cassidy followed Ty's instructions and brought Jasmine into the Blackout Headquarters. The guard at the gate waved them through, and a few minutes later they pulled up to a back entrance of the Daniel Oliver Building.

Hunter Bancroft, another operative, met them there and ushered them to a room on the third floor.

Ty waited inside for them.

"Everything go according to plan?" His gaze locked with Cassidy's.

Cassidy nodded, her hand on Jasmine's arm,

almost as if she were escorting a prisoner. She reminded herself that she wasn't.

"So far so good," Cassidy murmured.

"Ty . . ." Jasmine tugged out of Cassidy's grasp and stepped forward as if she might hug him, but then she stopped. Instead, her arms dropped to her side. "Cassidy said you were hurt."

"I'm fine." Ty crossed his arms over his chest as if not wanting to give her the wrong idea. "And I'm glad you're okay, Jasmine. But I have a lot of questions for you. Cassidy, will you please lock the door?"

Cassidy nodded and engaged the lock.

"This place looks secure. Why are you being so secretive?" Caution edged Jasmine's voice as she glanced around the room.

"We're being extra careful, especially until we know who we can trust."

Jasmine frowned, but her gaze turned icy. "Okay. Why are you looking at me like I'm the enemy?"

"I have some questions that I need answers to," Ty continued. "There's a lot at stake here. Your life isn't the only one on the line."

Cassidy fully planned to stay to hear this conversation. But her phone buzzed.

It was Doc Clemson.

Someone had come into the clinic a few moments

ago complaining of stomach pain. He'd been out surfing earlier in the day.

She frowned. "I need to check on this."

"Of course." Ty's gaze lingered on her before he nodded. "Check in later."

She nodded, disappointed to miss Jasmine's explanations. Cassidy could pass Doc Clemson's call off to one of her officers, but she didn't want to. She knew the ramifications of this sickness could be ugly given everything that had happened on the island recently.

She glanced at Jasmine and then at Ty before nodding. "I'll be back."

Ty was capable and trustworthy. He had a handle on this.

But her gut twisted with regret as she stepped away.

CHAPTER
TWENTY-FIVE

TY LOWERED himself into the chair across from Jasmine and swallowed hard. "I'm glad you're safe now."

"I'm sorry I ran. I was frightened." Jasmine glanced at her hands in her lap, her eyes shifting nervously.

"Rightfully so."

"They stabbed you because of me, didn't they?" Her voice cracked as she pulled her gaze to meet Ty's. "Ravi ordered it. Or did he do it himself?"

At her words, the wound in Ty's side began to ache. He tried not to show his discomfort, however. He didn't want anything to distract from the conversation. "It doesn't matter. It wasn't your fault."

"Ravi is targeting *you* because of *me*. He's going after you as revenge." Jasmine's gaze locked with his, deep emotion welling there. "I am sorry. I never intended for any of this to happen."

Ty broke his gaze with her and shifted, not wanting to get too emotional. He didn't want the woman to feel any more bonded with him than she already did. They needed to stick with the facts. "How does Ravi know I helped you escape ten years ago?"

"I'm not sure. But somehow they found out. And they tracked me down." Her chin trembled.

Ty held back his frown. Something wasn't adding up.

How would Ravi have discovered Ty was involved? Was it simply because Ravi's men had discovered Jasmine's location after hacking into video footage and using facial recognition? Once they knew where she was, had someone followed Jasmine to Lantern Beach and put the pieces together?

He couldn't be sure, but it seemed like a longshot.

Ty leaned forward, elbows on his legs. "You've got to talk to me, Jasmine. What's going on? Who do you think sold you out? And why?" He felt certain she knew more than she was saying.

"Why?" She let out a bitter laugh. "For money. It's always for money."

"It is a lot of times, that's for sure." Ty had seen it

enough to know it was a possibility. Though he hated to think about someone with the government doing so, it could have happened. "But who would do this?"

"I only kept in touch with my handler, Stanley, and the only person Stanley kept in touch with was Donaldson. I can only assume it was one of them. But Stanley is dead now . . . murdered." Her voice cracked.

Ty hadn't met Jasmine's handler. But he remembered Donaldson mentioning that two men who were part of her detail were dead and another in critical condition.

Who would have the most to gain in exposing Jasmine?

Donaldson's image slammed into Ty's mind.

Could the captain have something to do with this? Had the man been coerced or bribed into giving Ravi information? Was that how he'd afforded that new luxury waterfront home?

Ty didn't like the thought that this might be true.

What was he missing?

Then he remembered the photo Cassidy had found.

The picture of a boy who was the same age as Jasmine's son would be.

Ty turned to Jasmine and sucked in a deep breath

as he braced himself for what he knew would be an emotional conversation.

———

Cassidy stopped by the clinic and talked to the surfer who'd fallen ill.

His name was Gilbert Murphy. The fifty-some-thing man was practically a surfing legend on the island. He'd taught an uncountable number of people how to catch waves—while teaching them other various life lessons in the process.

Sure enough, despite the closed beach, he'd been surfing anyway—all in the same general area the fish kill had happened. One of his friends had been with him, and the friend reported feeling ill also. But he hadn't come to the clinic yet, citing he wanted to try treating his symptoms on his own.

The health department would need to make an official report.

The beach would have to remain closed until further notice.

This confirmed Cassidy's feelings that something was amiss.

Something unnatural.

Which was why she and Dillinger headed to Ocean Essence now.

She tried to get her thoughts off Jasmine and everything going on at Blackout. For the moment, at least. Ty and the gang were handling that situation, and there was little else Cassidy could do in the meantime.

"What do you hope to find out from Ocean Essence?" Dillinger asked as they headed down the road.

"I need to figure out if anyone there is involved in this. A lot of things are still uncertain. But my first step right now is to talk to them. There's a chance the company is dumping something toxic into our waterways."

"You really think they'd do that?" Dillinger did a doubletake at her. "It seems like people working at the lab would be smarter than that."

"They should be. As I'm sure you know, the marshes are vitally important to the health of our waterways. They help filter everything before it gets to the ocean or before it gets to any bodies of water. The animals living in that habitat are also valuable resources to us. Think about the fisherman and crabbers and what a loss to our economy that would be if they weren't able to bring in a haul every day."

"This is serious," Dillinger said. "I get it. You won't hear any arguments from me. Plus, it's against the law to dump chemicals. This lab is part of a large, international company. They know better. If they're guilty, they need to be held accountable."

"The problem will be finding evidence . . ." Cassidy's lips tugged down in a frown.

"Do you know anyone who works there?"

The image of a new friend filled her mind. "As a matter of fact, I do. And I won't hesitate to talk to her if I need to. But I'd like to leave her out of this for as long as possible—for her own well-being."

Cassidy and Dillinger pulled up to the lab. The two-story building was state of the art and privately nestled beside the Pamlico Sound. Titus, a Blackout agent, stood guard outside. Cassidy waved hello as she passed.

After parking, she and Dillinger strode inside. She hadn't called in advance to tell anyone she was coming, and she hoped that worked in her favor. The element of surprise could be a great interrogation tactic.

A cheery receptionist greeted them as they approached the desk. "How can I help you?"

"I need to talk to Dr. Hensley." Cassidy flashed her badge at the woman.

Her smile slipped. "I'm sorry, but Dr. Hensley has already left for the day."

"Is that right? How about Mr. Gains?" Lloyd Gains was the vice president of the company.

"I'm sorry, but Mr. Gains is out of town this week." The receptionist frowned apologetically again.

Those two men were the contacts Cassidy usually spoke with at the lab. No one else would be allowed to talk under the NDA they'd signed before starting with the company.

Cassidy fought a frown. Driving out here appeared to be a bust.

Her gaze met the receptionist's. "Please tell them I stopped by and that I need to talk with them first thing in the morning."

"Will do." The receptionist flashed another smile before jotting down a note.

Cassidy and Dillinger stepped outside.

"If it makes you feel better, I'm sure they wouldn't be forthright in offering any information anyway," Dillinger muttered.

"You're probably right. These laboratories are highly regulated. It looks like I'm going to have to make a few phone calls and bring someone in from the EPA to check this out too."

The door opened behind them, and Cassidy turned.

Rachel Atwood stepped out, her gaze focused on them. The woman was a scientist at the laboratory and had been vital in bringing down an employee who'd tried to sell proprietary information a couple of months ago.

The two of them were becoming friends, and Cassidy knew she could trust the woman.

But she didn't want to get her in trouble either.

"Cassidy, I saw you outside my window. Is everything okay?" Rachel's gaze skittered to Cassidy's.

Cassidy lowered her voice. "I believe the lab may be dumping toxic material. Sodium laureth sulphate, to be exact. We have two sick surfers, not to mention the fish kills happening on the island."

Rachel gasped and stepped closer. "We *do* use that chemical here. But I can't imagine anyone I work with dumping the substance in the water or marshes. There would be no reason to do that. We have the means at hand to dispose of it properly."

That raised an excellent point. Why *would* someone dispose of chemicals illegally when they had an adequate system in place?

Unless they were benefiting from it somehow.

Or hiding something.

"It's funny that you came by here asking about this because some animal rights activist stopped by earlier," Rachel continued.

"Was she an Asian woman with oversize glasses?" Cassidy already knew the answer to that question.

"Yes. That was her."

"Her name is Sierra, and she's with Paws and Furballs, an animal rights agency. I've talked to her already."

Rachel glanced nervously at the building as if checking to make sure no one was watching. "We had to have security run her off. She was on the property near the marshes doing something."

"Taking water samples," Cassidy muttered.

Rachel frowned as she processed what Cassidy said. "Listen, I don't want to think that something illegal is going on. But, if there is, whoever is behind it is going to try to cover their tracks. I'll do some asking around in here to see what I can find out."

"I'd appreciate that, but I don't want you to get yourself in trouble."

"I won't. I'll be careful. I promise."

But was being careful enough? Not if the stakes were too high.

Cassidy's back muscles tightened at the thought.

CHAPTER
TWENTY-SIX

LEAVING OCEAN ESSENCE, Cassidy headed to her cottage. She wanted to see for herself if there was any evidence her officers might have missed from Ty's attack.

She felt confident in her team, but she also wanted to put her own eyes on the scene. Plus, there was a chance her security cameras may have picked up on something. If so, she wanted to see what.

She pulled beneath her house and parked, Dillinger still with her.

Part of her wanted to do this alone. It was easier to keep secrets when she was by herself. But she'd promised Ty she'd be careful. Besides, she *did* feel better having someone else here with her.

As soon as she opened her SUV door, a horrible stench hit her.

She knew right away what it was.

Fish. Dead, decaying fish.

She and Dillinger exchanged a glance before bypassing the house and climbing the dune.

Sure enough, on the shore in the distance were hundreds and hundreds of fish, just like the ones that washed up near the lighthouse.

"Are these all up and down the beach or just here and by the lighthouse?" Dillinger wore a pinched expression as if the smell was getting to him.

"That's a good question," Cassidy said. "But I don't know. If they were everywhere, then I'd have to assume people would have called them in already. I'm sure the ocean current dictates where they might wash ashore. I'll place a call to NOAA and see what direction this all could be coming from."

"I'd say we have something else we need to worry about also," Dillinger muttered.

She shoved her eyebrows together at his ominous words. "What's that?"

He nodded toward her house, and she turned.

The breath left her lungs when she saw six red scarves tied around all the various posts.

Terror raced through her.

Someone was clearly trying to send a message— and to scare her.

And it had worked.

"Elijah," Jasmine muttered as she stared at the picture.

"Are you sure this is him?" Ty glanced at the photo as Jasmine grasped it in her trembling hands.

Tears filled her eyes. "I am. I keep up with him. I know I shouldn't. But how can I not? I miss him so much."

Ty's heart panged with compassion. He understood how hard it must have been to give him up. But she'd also agreed to let the boy go, to have no contact with him as a matter of safety. She'd made her choice and promised to stay away.

What other rules had she broken?

"Have you ever considered maybe that's how Ravi's guys found you?" Ty studied her face.

Her skin paled. "They don't know about Elijah."

"Are you sure?"

"If they knew, they'd abduct him. I would have heard."

Ty couldn't argue. If Ravi knew he had a child, he'd do everything in his power to bring him "home."

Or Ravi could use the child as bait, knowing that Jasmine was probably keeping tabs on the boy.

Ty frowned as he tried to think it through.

"I never meant to bring trouble here." Jasmine stared at Ty, both curiosity and regret in her gaze. "I know you have a life here. A child of your own. With my handler gone, I just didn't know who else to turn to."

His gaze latched onto hers. "Is there anything you're not telling me, Jasmine?"

She stared at him a moment, and Ty waited for whatever she had to say.

CHAPTER
TWENTY-SEVEN

"THERE'S *WHAT*?" Ty stared at Cassidy as they talked in the apartment at Blackout.

Dillinger had dropped her off and then gone to help Leggott place signs to close the beach after the fish kill.

Jasmine was safe with Hunter.

Ty's parents had gone to grab something to eat downstairs, and it was nice to have some time alone, if even for a few minutes.

Ty put together a cracker and cheese board, and he and Cassidy stood around the kitchen island munching on it.

Cassidy bounced Faith on her hip as she grabbed two crackers—one for herself and one for her daughter. "Unfortunately, you heard me correctly. There were six red scarves tied on the front of our house, left around various posts along our deck and exterior stairs."

His head began to pound. "I can't believe this."

Someone was definitely trying to send a message. A deadly message.

They were making it clear that both Ty and Cassidy were in their crosshairs.

Ty hated the helpless feeling that swept over him.

"I don't like this, Cassidy." He ran a hand through his hair. He wanted more than anything to get out of this building and do something.

But he couldn't do that yet. Doc Clemson said he needed more time to recover. He was tempted to forget the doctor's advice and do whatever he wanted. But he was also trying to remain levelheaded.

"I don't like any of this either." Cassidy stared at him.

He glanced at the cheese and cracker board, trying to figure out what to grab. But he didn't have an appetite. He felt too stirred up.

"If I had to guess, Ravi's men are coming and going from the island as they please," he finally said instead.

Cassidy's lips flicked as if she fought a frown. "At least, we know where Jasmine is now."

"Do you really think she may not be telling the

truth?" Ty's gaze locked with Cassidy's. He truly wanted to know her opinion.

"I think it's only wise to keep our eyes wide open right now."

"I think you're right."

"What about Captain Donaldson and the two guys he brought with him?" Cassidy nibbled on her cracker.

Ty felt his jaw tighten. "I don't trust them."

"Is there a specific reason? Or a gut feeling?"

"I don't know," Ty admitted. "It was something about their gazes. They were shifty. They know more than they're telling me."

Cassidy narrowed her eyes and held Faith a little closer. "Where are they now?"

"Colton is talking to them and buying some time. The truth is, Donaldson and his men don't have any better methods for finding Jasmine than we did. They're using manpower. I suppose the real reason they're here is so they can be close when she is discovered."

"Do you think they'll try to take Jasmine into custody?" Concern laced her words, and she grabbed another cracker for Faith, who made no secret she wanted another as she reached for the board in front of them.

"Not if they don't know she's here."

Cassidy's expression tightened. "We're walking a dangerous line here, Ty."

"I know." Ty's spine stiffened.

"I hope she's trustworthy. I hope she's worth the risk."

"We can't just hand her over to them. We don't know what Donaldson really wants from her."

"I understand." Cassidy still looked unconvinced, however.

As her phone rang, she muttered, "It's the FBI. Maybe they have an update."

———

Cassidy put the phone to her ear and listened as Agent Chen came over the line.

"As we've been investigating the death of the man outside of Blackout Headquarters, we found something today that you are going to want to see."

Her spine stiffened at the ominous words. "What's that?"

"I think it would be better if you came down to the police station so we can show you in person."

"Okay. I'll be right there."

Cassidy ended the call and told Ty what had happened.

"I want to go with you," Ty said.

"Is that a good idea?"

"I won't push myself. I'll just go for a ride with you."

She studied him another moment, trying to figure out the best plan of action. Finally, she nodded. "Okay then. As long as you promise to play it safe and don't take any chances."

"Me? Take chances? You must have me confused with someone else."

Cassidy gave him a look that spoke volumes.

Ty's parents returned from lunch, and Cassidy handed Faith over to Ty's mom.

A few minutes later, they were in Ty's truck—since Dillinger had taken her SUV. Cassidy drove since Ty was still on painkillers.

As they headed down the road, her thoughts spun out of control. What could the FBI have possibly found? Whatever it was, she hoped it led them to more answers, that it led them to finding Ravi and the men who were doing this here on the island.

She pulled into the police station, and they hurried inside. Chen and his team waited for her in the conference room, Chen with an almost annoyed look on his face. Then again, that was nothing new. Annoyed seemed to be his normal.

"You remember my husband, Ty," Cassidy

started. "I hope it's okay that he's here also."

She certainly wasn't going to send him away.

Chen studied Ty a moment, not bothering to hide his scrutiny.

"It's fine. In fact, I'm glad you're both here." He tapped something on the table. It looked like a series of photos. "You're going to want to see these."

Cassidy stepped closer and peered at whatever it was he was talking about.

She wasn't sure what she was expecting. But what she saw took her breath away.

They were surveillance photos.

Images of Cassidy at the Ocean Essence office talking to Rachel earlier today. Of Cassidy and Mac talking outside the luxury oceanfront rental after fire destroyed it. Of Ty and Cassidy at the police station.

Her gaze met Chen's. "Where did you get these?"

Chen twisted his neck almost as if he'd been hoping she would ask. "That's the other thing I wanted to talk to you about."

CHAPTER
TWENTY-EIGHT

TY LISTENED CAREFULLY, anxious to hear what Chen had to say.

"We found a camp set up in the woods not far from the lighthouse." Chen stood stiffly in Cassidy's office, his voice all business.

"What?" Cassidy's voice climbed in pitch. "Like a tent site?"

"Not exactly. We don't believe anyone was sleeping there. It appears the area was simply a place where these men were meeting to plan their evil deeds and reconvene."

"So more like a clandestine worksite." Cassidy crossed her arms, making it clear that update didn't make her happy.

"Exactly. We looked around for any evidence but left everything as it was," Chen continued. "I have two guys stationed there to keep an eye on the area in case the men come back."

"Who are 'these men'?" Cassidy raised her head as she waited for his answer.

"That's what we're trying to figure out." Chen paused. "Do you have any idea why someone would be watching you?"

Cassidy shrugged. "I *am* the police chief, and Ty is a former Navy SEAL. There are any number of reasons why someone could be watching us."

Chen nodded toward Ty. "We heard about the attack on you yesterday. This should have been reported to us."

Ty touched his side as he remembered being taken by surprise. He stopped the frown before it could form on his face. "It's been a whirlwind, to say the least. You think that what happened to me is connected with the man found beheaded outside of the Blackout Headquarters?"

"It's a good possibility. Unless things like this happen all the time on the island . . ." Chen flicked his gaze to them as if silently asking for confirmation.

Ty and Cassidy exchanged a glance. They both wanted to deny that things like this happened on the island often. But neither of them could.

For centuries, this swath of sand had attracted

pirates, adventurers, daredevils who weren't afraid to live in a rugged, isolated place.

Some things never changed. The faces and time period were different. But the overall danger remained.

"Mr. Chambers, was there any time when you were working as a SEAL when your missions may have taken you to Sahili?" Chen stared at him and waited for his answer.

"Sahili?" Ty rubbed his chin, careful not to show his surprise. "I did a lot of work in the Middle East."

Chen shifted. "But what about Sahili in particular?"

"Is that where this man was from? Do you know his name?" Ty continued to play it cool, careful not to give away too much. But if he could find out more information in the process . . .

Chen raised a hand. "Let's not get ahead of ourselves right now. I'm the one asking questions."

"I didn't have any direct missions to Sahili, though many of our missions were connected with various countries in the Middle East." Ty's words were mostly true. His assignment concerning Jasmine had been off the books. No one would find any evidence of it if they went searching. "Anything else you need to know, you're going to have to go above me. My work was classified."

"I would hate for something that was 'classified' to end up causing more people harm here on the island."

Guilt pounded at Ty. He would hate that also. But his hands were tied right now. He didn't want to disobey an order that had been given to him—especially if he didn't know all the details.

"Is there anything else that you might be able to tell me?" Ty asked, still hoping for more information so he could piece the truth together.

Chen's gaze locked on his. "If either of you are the target of these men, then you're in grave danger."

———

Cassidy glanced at Ty, worried about his coloring. Chen had stepped out of the room, leaving just the two of them. She was happy for a moment alone.

"I'm going to get you back to Blackout," she told him. "I think you're underestimating the toll a knife wound and blood loss can have on the body. I need you to be okay. Faith and I both need you to be."

He nodded, his face taut as he glanced out the window.

Cassidy knew that conversation with Chen had bothered him. She understood why.

His past was catching up with him. It was a hazard of the job.

A few minutes later, the two of them left to head back to Blackout.

As soon as they walked inside headquarters, Colton met them at the door. "I was hoping you'd be back here soon."

Cassidy and Ty both glanced around, looking for a sign that might indicate why Colton's voice sounded so urgent.

"Is it Donaldson?" Ty asked. "Did something happen with him?"

"No, he and his men are searching the island right now."

Cassidy released the breath she held. At least, those guys hadn't realized Jasmine was actually hiding at Blackout. That fact still made her apprehensive.

"So what's going on?" Ty remained bristled as if anticipating trouble.

"Come see for yourself." Colton nodded toward a conference room.

Finley looked up as they walked into the room, her glasses perched on the end of her nose and hair tumbling from her ponytail. Clearly, she'd been hard at work.

Cassidy's heart beat harder with anticipation.

Finley held up something small using some tweezers. "I found this buried in the drone."

"What is it?" Ty stepped closer.

"It's a small slip of paper, probably the same size as you might find your fortune on in a fortune cookie. It was placed in the drone on purpose."

"What's on it?" Cassidy's lungs tightened as she anticipated what may have been left there.

"Apparently, these guys suspected that you would take down the drone. They wanted to send you a message."

"Don't keep us in suspense anymore," Ty said.

Finley carefully opened the paper using her tweezers and held it in front of her. She hesitated before starting. "The message says, 'You're going to pay.'"

Cassidy's throat went dry at the words.

CHAPTER
TWENTY-NINE

IT WAS GETTING LATE, and Ty had a lot on his mind.

Cassidy had to take some phone calls. Several more people were ill on the island, and Ty suspected it had something to do with the water.

While she did that, he went to go check on Jasmine.

When he stepped into the room, it appeared Jasmine had showered. Her hair was still damp, and she wore some clean jeans and a sweatshirt that Cassidy had brought her. However, her eyes still contained that forlorn, sunken expression.

"How are you holding up?" Ty pulled a chair over and straddled it in front of her. The back of the chair created a nice barrier between them.

He was fully aware that Jasmine was attracted to him. That she was lonely and needed someone.

But Ty wasn't that guy.

He needed to put as much distance between them as he could.

"I feel like being here is like being in prison." She shrugged and picked at a blanket in front of her as if needing a distraction.

"I'm sorry you feel that way. I'm sure it's frustrating. A prison isn't what we intended. We only need to keep you safe."

Her face twitched as if she wanted to argue with his statement.

She didn't.

Instead, she glanced at the window.

"Was that Donaldson I saw outside earlier?" A vein popped out at her temple at the question. Clearly, the man's presence made her anxious—and for good reason.

She'd been through a lot, and knowing who to trust in these situations was difficult, to say the least.

Ty nodded, knowing better than to hold back the truth from her. "He doesn't know you're here."

"Do you not trust him?" Jasmine studied Ty, her gaze searching for the truth in his eyes, in his body language. The woman was smart and observant.

Of course, she'd realize there was more here than met the eye. But Ty still needed to be careful how much he shared.

His gut clenched as he considered his words. "I don't know who to trust right now."

Jasmine let out a long sigh, almost as if disappointed with his answer. Finally, she admitted, "Me neither."

"He *is* the one who can help you start a new life somewhere. He has those resources."

"Or he could be the one who led Ravi to me." Her bottom lip stuck out in a pout.

Ty swallowed hard but didn't deny her words. Jasmine could be right, and there was no reason to make her feel otherwise.

Instead, he asked, "Have you remembered anything else that could help us?"

He carefully watched her expression.

Something glimmered in her gaze.

She did have something on her mind, didn't she?

Ty held his breath as he waited to hear what she would say.

————

Cassidy stole a few more minutes with Faith.

It was getting late, but she couldn't resist the extra time with her daughter. However, it didn't take long for Faith's eyes to close.

She gently placed Faith in her crib and then stepped out of the room. Ty's parents were already asleep. Cassidy knew they were exhausted, but she was so grateful for all their help. She wouldn't be able to do her job right now without them.

She walked toward the sliding door on the exterior wall and opened it. Not all the apartments here at the Daniel Oliver Building had balconies. But this one had a small one, and she could use some fresh air right now.

She stepped outside, and a cool evening breeze washed over her. She closed her eyes, relishing the wind as it kissed her skin.

Her thoughts wandered to Ty.

She didn't like the thought of him being with Jasmine. But she trusted him. Seeing Faith had been more important than babysitting the situation.

Her head pounded at the thought of everything that had happened. At the moment it felt like it would be impossible to reconcile the criminal activities that had occurred here on the island with the truth. No matter which way Cassidy tried to push the details together, nothing fit in a way that made sense.

She'd be happy when this was resolved and life returned to normal. Although she had to say that life as police chief here on Lantern Beach was hardly ever boring.

As Cassidy opened her eyes, she scanned the water in the distance and the edge of the woods that backed up to it. The landscape really was a beautiful sight to behold—peaceful.

This property was the perfect location for Blackout. The people working here needed a place to unwind between their missions. Plus, it was now filled with families and children.

A shout echoed through the air.

Instantly, Cassidy glanced up at the sky.

Had another drone been spotted?

Only a clear sky stared back.

But something was definitely stirring in the air.

She peered around the property but didn't see anything from her vantagepoint.

More voices sounded in the distance.

Then her radio beeped.

She grabbed it and listened to the garbled voices on the transmission. As she did, she briskly walked inside and closed the sliding door, careful to lock it behind her. Then she darted from the apartment and headed downstairs.

"It's Beckett . . ." a deep voice said. "He's been . . . stabbed."

Her lungs froze.

Another Blackout member had been attacked?

Dread filled her. This couldn't be happening.

CHAPTER
THIRTY

TY STOOD near where Beckett had been injured. Cassidy was investigating the scene, but she'd already called the FBI, knowing they'd want to see the scene themselves.

Ty had decided to mention this to Donaldson, but the man currently wasn't answering his phone.

Paramedics had already arrived to tend to Beckett.

He'd been stabbed once in his side—the same exact place Ty had been wounded.

By the time the other guard got to him, he was unconscious.

Ty pressed his eyes together and prayed. Prayed for his friend's well-being. Prayed for everyone who might be in danger. The list seemed extensive right now.

From what Ty gathered, Beckett had heard a noise on the outside perimeter of the property. He'd told his colleagues he was going to check it out.

Somewhere in that process, someone had lunged from behind a tree. The man's knife had sliced into Beckett's side.

But this time, the assailant had twisted his weapon, causing even more damage and blood loss.

And he'd left a feather.

Ty's stomach turned at the thought.

Ty had already called Beckett's girlfriend, Samantha Reynolds. She was on her way to the island now.

He hated making calls like that. Absolutely hated it.

This man had to be stopped.

Ty refused to stand here and do nothing.

He searched for something he could do to help.

He glanced up and saw the surveillance camera on the side of the building.

He needed to check that.

Now.

If Cassidy wanted to see this and examine it for herself, this was the best moment to do so. The FBI would be here at any minute, and they might try to push her out of the investigation again.

He paced over toward Cassidy. "We need to look at the security footage."

Cassidy rose from the grass where she'd been searching for footprints. "I could use a break from this. Let's go inside and look at it. I'll leave my officers to keep looking until the FBI arrives."

While paramedics continued to treat Beckett, Cassidy and Ty went to check out the video.

On the way inside, Ty motioned for Colton to join them, and Colton followed them into Ty's office.

A few minutes later, Ty pulled up the footage on his computer, and they all watched the screen.

"Right there." Colton pointed at the grainy footage. "This is when it happened."

Ty rewound the video a few seconds and then hit Play again.

They all watched with bated breath as Beckett walked along the outside perimeter of the campus.

As he stepped toward the woods, a figure jumped out from behind a tree. Beckett bristled and reached for his gun. Before he could grab it, the man thrust a knife into his side. Beckett fell to the ground.

Beckett couldn't have even seen it coming.

The man then proceeded to kick Beckett in the side and face.

Disgust swirled inside Ty.

"Can you zoom in on those final images?"

Cassidy squinted as she studied the screen, acting as if she may have missed something.

"Let me see what I can do." Ty enlarged the still frames to see if they could make out any features of the man who'd stabbed him.

The man's shadowed features became clearer.

That's when Ty felt the breath leave his lungs.

"What is it?" Cassidy glanced at him, searching his gaze for answers.

"That man . . . I can't be sure . . ." Ty's throat went dry as he stared at the frozen image. "But he almost looks like . . . Ravi Jabal."

———

The FBI arrived on scene ten minutes later.

Just as Cassidy expected, Chen announced they were taking over this investigation. In fact, not only were they taking over, but Chen essentially banned Cassidy from interfering.

Anger churned inside her at his arrogant declaration. Cassidy didn't *interfere*. She investigated. However, she knew there was nothing she could do about Chen's decision.

Not officially, anyway.

Compliance was the best choice right now—at least, she needed to *seem* compliant.

There was no way she was walking away from what had happened to Beckett.

Cassidy turned back to her guys, careful to maintain her composure. "You heard Agent Chen. You're both relieved of duty from this case."

Dillinger and Bradshaw gave her lingering glances full of questions—and a touch of outrage.

"Yes, Chief," Dillinger finally said with a stiff voice.

Both men turned to walk away.

She needed to talk to them away from any listening ears.

Before her officers got too far away, she jogged toward them. "Wait up."

When the three of them were out of earshot, Bradshaw stopped and turned toward her. His gaze was lit with fire and determination.

"Are you just going to let them take over like that?" he asked in a harsh whisper.

Cassidy didn't like his tone, but she didn't correct him. She understood how frustrating this situation felt. "I don't like this any more than you do."

"Why aren't you fighting this? It's not like you . . ." Dillinger's hands went to his hips as he waited for her answer.

"Exactly," Cassidy said. "Allowing those bozos to take over on my watch is not something I would do. I'm still looking into this—I'm just not playing by the FBI's rules. But they don't have to know that."

Dillinger nodded as realization seemed to roll over his features. "Gotcha. That makes more sense. I thought you were losing your fight there for a minute, and you had me worried."

"I'm just trying to look agreeable. For now, at least." Her gaze flicked back and forth between the two of them. "In the meantime, I'm going to need both of you guys to be on guard. Beckett is one of the best. So is Ty. These men have gotten to both of them. I don't want to see anything like that happen to either of you."

"We'll be careful, boss," Bradshaw said. "You watch out for yourself also."

"I will. Now I need to talk to Ty. We need to figure a few things out."

"Just let us know what you need," Bradshaw said. "We'll get out of here and handle things on the island."

She nodded and walked back toward the building, where Ty waited for her. As soon as they got inside and away from any listening ears, Cassidy let down her guard.

"I don't like this, Ty," she murmured.

"I don't either. Listen, we didn't have a chance to

talk earlier, but you'll never believe what Jasmine told me."

Cassidy's heartbeat quickened as they paused near the stairway in the lobby. With Beckett being stabbed, she'd almost forgotten Ty had visited the woman.

"What's that?" she asked.

"Jasmine said, when she was back in Canada before running, she went to talk to members of her security detail. One particular guard—Hurst was his last name—was on duty. She walked in on him while he was on the phone with someone."

"And?" Her heart pulsed in her ears as she waited to see where this was going.

"Hurst said my name."

"What?" Surprise laced her voice as she processed this bombshell.

Ty shrugged and glanced around.

No one else was nearby.

He continued, "No one was supposed to know I was involved. So I don't know how this guy got my information."

Her gut tightened. She didn't like the sound of this. Didn't like the fact that some stranger had known Ty was connected to Jasmine.

No one outside the operation was supposed to know.

"What else did Jasmine hear?" she asked.

"That's the thing." Ty frowned. "The guy turned and saw Jasmine standing there, so he cut the conversation short. She doesn't know anything else."

"So maybe this Hurst guy is the one who's the traitor?"

"Maybe. He's still unable to talk right now. Maybe once he wakes up, we'll learn more."

"I hope so. Because I want answers."

Ty rubbed his jaw as their gazes locked. "Believe me, so do I."

CHAPTER
THIRTY-ONE

THE NEXT MORNING, Agent Chen and his men called a meeting with Donaldson, Ty, and Cassidy. Ty insisted on having it at the Blackout Headquarters—on their turf.

He'd already been hard at work today—starting with checking on Beckett. His friend and colleague had been taken to a hospital in Raleigh and was in stable condition. The doctor expected a full recovery —which was such a relief.

Chen hadn't argued with Ty's request. But as soon as he'd arrived, he'd taken control and demanded an update from everyone.

"Maybe we should bring Donaldson up to speed on what happened last night first." Ty gave Chen a pointed look and then the captain.

Donaldson had never called Ty back last night.

Where had the captain been? What was going on? He needed to find out.

But first, Ty shared what had happened to Beckett.

"I'm sorry to hear that," Donaldson muttered, his frown growing larger. The expression had started the moment Chen tried to take charge.

Donaldson had never liked it when other people treaded on his territory.

"Speaking of which, I was expecting a call back from you." Ty narrowed his eyes as he studied the captain.

"We had another matter to attend to, unfortunately."

"What kind of matter?" Ty asked.

Donaldson's icy glare met his. "I can't tell you any details."

"If you and your men know something that might put the people here on this island in danger, then you need to tell us." Cassidy bristled as she stared at the captain, her tone leaving no room for argument.

"It wasn't pertaining to what's going on here." Donaldson glowered at Cassidy.

"Does someone want to fill me in on exactly what's happening right now?" Chen stared down everyone in the room from his position at the head of the table.

Ty and Cassidy said nothing, leaving the response in Donaldson's hands.

Finally, the captain sighed and filled Chen in on the Jasmine situation.

"This would have been good to know earlier." Chen muttered several unflattering things beneath his breath before pulling himself together. "It suddenly makes sense why Ravi Jabal might be on the island. Has anybody had any luck locating Jasmine?"

Most people shook their heads. Ty and Cassidy remained quiet.

"So you have no idea where she is now?" Chen reiterated.

"We discovered she was staying on a yacht," Ty admitted. "But we lost her after that."

"What about the man who was found beheaded near Blackout?" Cassidy's gaze zeroed in on Chen. "Any updates on him?"

Ty was thankful for the change in topic.

Chen's gaze darkened. "We don't have any leads on who killed him or what his identity is."

"So basically, you've taken over the investigation, but you've gotten nowhere." Cassidy's voice sounded pointed.

Atta girl. Ty held back his smile. He loved his wife's spunk—loved so much about her, for that matter. His life was richer because she was in it. He would fight with everything inside him to make sure it stayed that way.

Chen scowled again. "We're working to find answers and believe we'll have some soon."

"So what do you want from us?" Cassidy stared at him.

Chen crossed his arms, appearing unyielding as he stood in front of them. "Just information. I expect you to share whatever you find."

Ty didn't like his tone or the way Chen didn't include the rest of them.

He glanced at Donaldson. Based on his scowl, the captain wasn't happy either.

But why wasn't he arguing? Fighting more? Being territorial as usual?

Ty couldn't be sure.

But he felt certain there were things the captain wasn't sharing with him.

Deadly things, perhaps.

Chen's gaze locked with Ty's. "Are you sure you don't know where Jasmine is?"

Silence stretched as Ty thought about his response.

————

Cassidy waited to see what Ty would say.

Would he admit that Jasmine was in their custody? That the woman was staying right here probably only three hundred feet away from where they were meeting?

Cassidy wasn't sure how he would handle this situation—but he'd make the right choice, she was sure.

Ty shrugged. "We're keeping our eyes open for her."

So he still didn't want anyone here to know about Jasmine's presence. Did he still not trust someone on this team? There was a good chance that was true.

Cassidy glanced around the table and wondered if someone in this room wasn't trustworthy. She didn't know any of them well enough to say.

But the fact that Jasmine's location had been discovered *did* seem suspicious, almost like there had to be an inside source who'd leaked those details. Plus, why had that one agent said Ty's name right before the attack?

As everyone talked amongst themselves, Donaldson's phone beeped, and he excused himself to take the call.

When he returned to the room a few minutes later, a new emotion filled his gaze.

Was that excitement? Did he have an update?

"Hurst is awake," he announced.

Hurst . . . the agent who'd said Ty's name.

Cassidy's pulse skipped a beat.

"Is he able to talk?" Ty bristled as he leaned forward, waiting for Donaldson's answer.

"They said he's lucid," Donaldson stated. "They're going to put him on a video call with us right now."

CHAPTER
THIRTY-TWO

TY HELD his breath as Agent Hurst came onto the screen at the front of the room.

The thirtysomething man had clearly been beaten up. His face was swollen and bruised, with various lacerations. He sat in a hospital bed, and his thick, dark hair looked greasy and his gown rumpled.

"Agent Hurst." Donaldson stood near the screen as if staking his claim as leader of the situation room. "First of all, we're glad to see that you're awake."

"Glad to be awake." Hurst's voice sounded hoarse and scratchy—almost hard to understand, which seemed expected for the situation. "Wasn't sure that was a possibility for a while."

"We were all waiting with bated breath for your recovery," Donaldson said. "I know you still have a long road ahead of you."

"That's what everyone is telling me."

Donaldson briefly introduced everyone in the room before getting to business. "I hate to cut to the chase, but time is of the essence right now. We would really like a detailed report on what happened before you were attacked. We're hoping you feel up for that."

"Yes, sir. Of course." Hurst nodded, though the action looked painful. "I was on duty, guarding the asset's house. She was concerned that her identity had been discovered."

"Had you seen any evidence of that?" Donaldson narrowed his eyes as he waited for Hurst's response.

"No, sir. But on this particular day, I thought I saw movement across the street. I started outside to check it out. As soon as I opened the door, a man jumped me. He stabbed me then went inside and killed my colleagues." Hurst's voice cracked as he no doubt fought horrible memories.

"Nothing suspicious happened before that?" Donaldson asked. "Anything to indicate how the asset might have been discovered?"

Hurst sucked in a breath. "As a matter of fact, there's been something I haven't been able to stop thinking about since I woke."

Ty held his breath as he anticipated what the man might say.

"And what is that?" Impatience tinged Donaldson's voice.

Hurst ran his hand through his hair as if he were uncertain how to say it.

Everyone waited, the room dead silent.

Hurst licked his lips before saying, "You're never going to believe this but—"

Before he could finish his statement, static filled the screen.

"Hurst?" Donaldson stepped closer. "Are you still there?"

Static continued to stretch across the monitor.

Ty hoped it would clear and that Hurst could finish what he was about to say.

Then the screen went black.

The call was lost, he realized.

The question was: had the call cut out on accident? Or had someone orchestrated the disconnect before Hurst could share valuable—and possibly incriminating—information?

————

Donaldson told everyone to take a thirty-minute break while one of his men tried to figure out what had happened to their connection and make sure

Hurst was okay. Ten minutes had already passed with no luck.

Ty thought the timing of the call ending was suspicious.

But Ty had no evidence to prove anything had been hacked. Still, something didn't sit right with him.

As Jasmine's image filled his mind, he rose.

He leaned toward Cassidy and whispered, "I'm going to check on Jasmine."

"I need to make some calls anyway. Two more people came to the clinic sick after swimming in the ocean. I just got a text about it." She frowned as she glanced at her phone.

Ty hurried upstairs and dismissed Hunter from guard duty for a few minutes. In case something was going on, Ty didn't want anything to raise suspicions, and a guard positioned in the hallway could be a red flag. Since Ty was inside, he could keep an eye on things for a few minutes.

Jasmine rose from the couch when Ty walked in, and her eyes lit as if she were excited to see him. "I was hoping you would stop by again."

He paused in front of her, wondering about the undertone of her words. "Is everything okay?"

She rubbed her arms and glanced at the window. "I just feel anxious. I'm tired of being here."

"You knew this was what your life would be like when you went into hiding." He hated to remind her of that fact, but his words were true. She hadn't chosen an easier life—but it was still far better than the one she'd left behind.

"I know, but . . ." Something seemed to switch in Jasmine, and she stepped closer. Her eyes softened as she rested her hand on his chest.

Ty gently pushed her away.

Jasmine's lips puckered, making it clear she didn't appreciate the action. "I only feel safe when you're with me. I know how that probably sounds. But it's true."

"I assure you that the guard we have assigned outside your door is very competent." He kept his tone even with no room for misunderstanding. He couldn't let Jasmine entertain the idea that the two of them could ever be together.

"I know he is, but . . . he's not you." Jasmine stared up at him, imploring him with her gaze.

"Jasmine . . ." Was he going to have to spell this out for her? That was how it appeared.

"I know you're married," she rushed. "But you were so kind and wonderful to me. Most men in my life are not like that."

His jaw tightened as he remembered the abuse she'd been through. "I'm sorry that's been your experience. I truly am. But we're going to have to put some boundaries in place. I want to help you, but I also don't want to give you the wrong idea. I'm here to help you, but only in a professional capacity."

She stared into his eyes, still not dissuaded. "Ty . . ."

He took a step back. "I can see that coming to check on you right now wasn't a good idea. I'll come back later when you're not so emotional."

He didn't want to dismiss her feelings or her fear. But Ty couldn't let this go on. The hero complex Jasmine felt toward him wasn't healthy.

"But Ty . . ."

"I'm sorry, Jasmine." He headed toward the door.

But when he opened it, Chen stood on the other side, an accusatory look in his eyes.

CHAPTER
THIRTY-THREE

CHEN PUSHED inside the room and closed the door behind him.

"I knew you were up to something." His gaze flickered behind Ty to Jasmine before narrowing as he turned back to Ty. "How long have you had her here? How long have you been lying to us?"

Ty's jaw tightened. He knew he was in a bad spot right now—but he'd known that would be the case when he'd brought Jasmine here. Everything he'd done had been of his own volition.

"It's not important how long she's been here," Ty muttered.

"I say it is. You've been impeding a federal investigation. I can arrest you right now for that."

"I'm just trying to keep her safe."

Chen narrowed his eyes. "I think that's what we're all trying to do."

Ty tried to choose his words carefully. "I'm not sure who we can trust right now. The only way Jasmine's identity could have been discovered was if there was someone on the inside."

Chen stared at him, his gaze dark and assessing—and laced with anger over Ty's betrayal. Nothing Ty had just said had gotten through to him. As far as Chen was concerned, Ty was now the enemy.

"I need to talk with Jasmine alone," Chen announced as he motioned toward the door. "Let's go."

"I won't go anywhere without Ty." Jasmine stepped closer, practically huddling behind Ty.

Ty's back muscles tightened, but he didn't argue. Despite the distance he wanted to put between himself and Jasmine, he didn't want her going anywhere without him either.

Chen's gaze skimmed back and forth again before he finally nodded. "Fine. But I'm not talking to you here."

"Why not?" Ty demanded. "It's secure here—more so than anywhere else on the island."

"It's not secure enough for me. I need to take you guys somewhere private."

"I think it's better that we stay here." Ty crossed

his arms, determined to keep Jasmine safe. Leaving this campus would be a major mistake.

In one swift motion, Chen grabbed his gun from the holster at his shoulder.

He pointed it directly at Ty. "I'm not going to ask you again. We're going to leave the Blackout campus, and you're going to drive exactly where I tell you to."

Wait . . . Chen was more than angry about Ty's deception, wasn't he?

Was Chen in on this?

Ty's heart pounded harder as the reality of the situation hit him. Ty had his gun on him, but the Glock was holstered at his waist. He could fight Chen in hand-to-hand combat, but this was a tight space and Ty's knife injury still bothered him.

It was too risky.

His best bet was to go along with Chen and look for a way of escape later.

Jasmine gripped his arm, her fear obvious.

Ty stared at Chen another moment, trying to figure out exactly what this man was thinking.

"Put your gun on the floor," Chen growled.

Ty gritted his teeth as he did exactly what Chen said. He was all too aware of the barrel of Chen's gun aimed right at him the whole time.

He and Jasmine would need to comply.

For now.

But this was far from being over.

———

Cassidy started down the hallway to go talk to Ty when she heard voices and paused.

She ducked around the corner before anyone saw her.

Something about the tone of the people talking instantly made her cautious.

Carefully, she peered around the corner to see what was happening.

Ty stepped from Jasmine's room, Jasmine behind him.

Chen followed.

Chen had found them! How had that happened? And what was he doing?

As Cassidy stole another glance, she saw the FBI agent was holding a gun.

Was he arresting Ty and Jasmine? Taking them into custody?

Her gut told her that wasn't the case.

Something else was going on here.

As the FBI agent glanced up and down the hallway, Cassidy ducked back behind the corner and out of sight. Her heart raced as she tried to formulate her next plan of action.

"This way," Chen muttered.

She peered around the corner again, trying to see which direction they might be heading.

They walked toward the stairway at the other end of the hallway.

Chen? Was he one of the bad guys? The one who'd sold Ty out?

That was the only explanation that made sense.

Cassidy's lungs tightened as she grabbed her phone and texted Colton.

She didn't know where Chen planned on taking Ty and Jasmine.

But she would follow, and she'd need backup—especially if Ravi was involved in this.

If she wanted to see Ty alive again, she'd have to be very careful.

The door to the stairway closed. She waited a few minutes before she followed.

She crept to the first floor in time to see the threesome step outside.

Chen casually—with his gun concealed beneath his jacket—led them to Ty's truck and motioned for him to get into the driver's seat. Jasmine sat in the middle and Chen on the other side.

A moment later, they took off toward the gate.

They were leaving Blackout.

Where could they be heading?

Cassidy considered calling the guard at the front gate and having him lock the place down.

But she didn't. That gate wouldn't slow Chen down. He'd blow through it. Someone might even be hurt in the process.

Her best bet was to take Chen by surprise.

She climbed into her personal car and cranked the engine, thankful she had her keys in her pocket.

Then she started carefully following behind, praying she didn't get sloppy and make any mistakes that would cost anyone their lives.

CHAPTER
THIRTY-FOUR

"WHERE ARE WE GOING?" Ty glanced from the corner of his eye at Chen as they headed down the road.

He noticed Jasmine trembling between them. He couldn't blame her for her fear.

He wasn't sure how this situation would turn out. He prayed for a good outcome. For wisdom and favor.

"You'll find out where we're going soon enough," Chen muttered.

Ty stared straight ahead at the island road. "Are you working for Ravi?"

"Stop asking questions." Chen readjusted the grip on his gun, making it clear he was growing irritated.

Ty's thoughts continued to race. Someone would

notice they were missing soon. Backup would search for them.

He just wasn't sure what might happen in the meantime.

"Keep going south," Chen muttered as they headed farther from Blackout Headquarters.

One main road cut through the middle of the town with many side roads branching out from it.

But this was the way to the docks. Would Chen try to put them on a boat and whisk them away?

Ty didn't think that would be the case. If anything, Chen would take them somewhere they could be transported via helicopter.

But had Chen thought this through enough to have organized that?

Ty didn't think so. Finding Jasmine at Blackout had caught him by surprise.

He was winging it right now.

Ty needed to use that to his advantage.

He gripped the steering wheel harder as his thoughts raced. Chen was a highly trained FBI agent.

But Ty's Navy SEAL training was better—at least when it came to all things tactical.

However, having Jasmine here made it more diffi-cult. Chen could use her as leverage.

She sniffled beside him, crying through her fear.

This never should have happened. Her location

should have never been discovered. These people should have never tracked her down.

The US government had promised to protect her. Instead, someone on the inside had betrayed her.

Anger burned through Ty at the thought.

"Turn here," Chen ordered.

Ty turned left into a driveway leading to a secluded house on the sound side of the island.

Had Ravi's guys been staying in this house the whole time? Ty didn't see any cars around. But enough woods surrounded the property that vehicles could be hidden.

As Ty put the truck into Park, a man stepped out the front door to greet them.

Ty's eyes widened as he recognized the figure.

Ravi Jabal.

Jasmine spotted him also and let out a cry of defeat.

———

Cassidy saw Ty's truck turn, and she put on her brakes. She grabbed her phone and called Colton with an update.

He and Axel were right behind her.

She'd been to this part of the island before and knew some small cabins were back in this area. The houses here were mostly unused except for a few times a year when people came down to fish.

She didn't pull into the driveway. Instead, she drove past it and pulled off the road. She parked her car behind the patch of woods at the edge of the property.

She couldn't take any chances.

Thankfully, Colton pulled in right behind her.

The three of them met in front of their vehicles, weapons drawn.

Cassidy knew she could trust the Blackout guys. They would have her back.

Donaldson? That remained unknown.

"What's our plan?" Axel paused beside her, his muscles bristled as if poised for action.

"We don't know what's going on inside that house," Colton said. "One wrong move, and Ty could be dead."

Cassidy's throat tightened at his words. She couldn't even entertain that thought. It would derail her if she did.

No, she had to stay positive. Had to believe everything would be okay.

"We need to get closer, see what's happening," she murmured.

"Let's think this through first." Colton frowned as

he stared through the woods. "As soon as these guys see us coming, they're going to act."

"You're right. But somehow, we have to get Ty out of there safely." Her voice cracked as emotions fought to emerge, to take control. "Jasmine too."

"Let's call more backup." Colton locked his gaze with hers. "Then we're going to undertake one of the most important missions of our lives."

Cassidy lifted a prayer.

Ty could be hurt . . . or worse.

A sob caught in her throat, and she pushed that thought down.

Cassidy would do whatever it took to protect him.

"How could Chen be involved in this?" She shook her head, still unable to comprehend it.

"Where there's money, there's betrayal. I've seen it too many times."

Cassidy couldn't deny Colton's words. She'd seen it also.

But as an image of what Ravi could do to Ty filled her mind, more fear began to creep in, and a sense of urgency nearly consumed her.

CHAPTER
THIRTY-FIVE

CHEN HELD onto Jasmine's arm as he shoved Ty forward with the barrel of his gun. "Keep moving."

Ty glanced up at Ravi and felt himself bristle. The man was around six feet tall with thick, dark hair and brooding eyes that almost looked as dark as obsidian. His nose was slightly crooked, and his eyebrows were shaggy.

Based on the smile on Ravi's face, the man was looking forward to punishing Ty.

Maybe Jasmine also.

Ty prayed for wisdom as Chen pushed him up the stairs.

"So, you're the man I've heard so much about," Ravi said in clipped English.

Ty kept his gaze even. "Have we met before?"

"Not directly." His smug voice—full of broken English—filled the air. "Yet I feel as if we know each other."

"Why did you bring me here?"

"Why did you abduct my wife?" Ravi's gaze flickered to Jasmine, and his scowl deepened.

"I don't know what you're talking about." Ty kept his expression neutral.

Ravi smacked his hand across Ty's face.

"Stop lying!" Spittle flew from the man's mouth as he barked the words.

Jasmine gasped, practically radiating fear.

Ty forced himself to remain upright, to not show any pain. He wouldn't give Ravi that pleasure, even if his jaw ached.

"I've been anticipating this day for years." Ravi stared at Ty with disgust. "Now the day has finally come."

If Ty could just keep this guy talking . . . maybe they'd stand a chance. Maybe backup would arrive to help him.

"That's a long time to hold a grudge," Ty murmured. "Let's just talk this through."

Ravi reached into his pocket and pulled out a knife.

The six-inch blade was jagged, curved, and clearly sharp.

Ty's throat tightened as he gazed at the weapon. He knew the man had plans for that knife. Plans that involved Ty.

At once, he remembered the searing pain from his recent stab wound. The memories tried to freeze him, but he couldn't let that happen. He had to be on his A-game right now.

Ty had to somehow disarm this man.

Chen still held a gun behind him, however.

It was too risky to make any moves right now. Ty would have to wait for the right opportunity.

Instead, he stood firmly where he was, making sure to remain in front of Jasmine.

So many things still didn't make sense.

Like . . . how had Chen even gotten involved with all of this?

"How can you sell out your country like this, Chen?" Ty asked the FBI agent, even as he kept his gaze on Ravi. "I never pictured you as a traitor."

When Chen didn't answer immediately, Ty turned just in time to see Jasmine twirl toward Chen.

Let out a guttural yell.

Grab his gun.

Then she pulled the trigger.

The bullet hit Chen in the chest.

The FBI agent's eyes widened with surprise before he groaned.

Then he tumbled down the steps.

His body hit the ground with a thud.

Ty's heart pounded as he watched everything unfold.

He glanced at Jasmine.

She still held the gun in her trembling hands.

But instead of pointing it at Ravi, the weapon was aimed at Ty.

————

Cassidy's phone buzzed in her pocket, and she grabbed it as she trekked through the small patch of woods with Colton and Axel.

Donaldson had texted her.

She quickly scanned what he wrote.

"You guys . . ." she started. "Apparently, there was a jammer in the conference room, and that's why we lost our signal. They just found it beneath a chair."

"A jammer?" Colton shook his head. "Who had a jammer?"

Someone who was trying to cover something up . . . the person who was the mole.

"Chen," she responded.

"What?" Colton's voice rose. "I can't believe that. What else did Donaldson say?"

She read his message again. "He was able to talk to Hurst a few minutes ago. Hurst said an FBI agent contacted him and told him to be on the lookout for . . . Ty."

"What?" Colton's surprise seemed to grow— along with his voice.

She shushed him.

Just then, a gunshot cut through the air.

Her heart lurched into her throat.

Ty . . . was he okay?

She glanced at Colton and saw the concern in his eyes also.

Their steps quickened as they hurried through the woods to the other property.

She tried not to anticipate the worst. But she knew how evil Ravi was. She knew he wanted others to suffer.

They cleared the woods in time to spot someone lying on the ground.

Cassidy sucked in a breath.

Was that . . . Chen?

Chen had been shot?

Cassidy scanned everything around the area.

If that was the case, then where was Ty right now?

Before she could think about that too long, something fell from the tree above her.

Not something.

Someone.

One of Ravi's guys.

Based on his grin, he was going to enjoy this fight.

CHAPTER
THIRTY-SIX

"ARE you ready to pay the price?" Ravi stared at Ty after Jasmine forced him inside the house.

Ty glared at the man. "This is really how you want to do this?"

"I've been imagining this day for years. *Years.*"

Ty's gaze flickered to Jasmine, who stood behind him, Chen's gun still in her trembling hands. "And you've been on in on this, Jasmine? Even after Ravi treated you the way he did?"

As they talked, Ravi grabbed some zip ties and secured Ty's wrists to the arms of a thick, wooden chair.

The panic on her face surprised him. He'd expected to see maliciousness or a more calculated look.

"He has Elijah." Tears welled in her eyes. "I had no choice. I'm so sorry."

More facts clicked into place in Ty's mind.

Ty turned his head toward Ravi. "How did you find out she had a son?"

"Once I found out where Jasmine was staying, I had my men search her computer and cell phone records. I wondered why she was keeping tabs on the boy. Then I saw a picture of him, and I knew he was mine. She'd kept me from my son."

Something about Ravi's tone made Ty certain that he wasn't going to walk away from the situation alive.

Not without some intervention, at least.

"Do you have the boy now?" Ty asked.

"Of course, I have what's mine."

Ty felt the blood drain from his face at the thought of this evil man ripping a child away from his family. "I see. Where is he?"

"That's not important." Ravi's voice hardened.

Cassidy's and Faith's images flashed in his mind.

What if Ty never saw them again? What if he left Faith fatherless and Cassidy widowed?

Nothing would make Ravi happier. He knew that.

But he also knew that he'd fight with everything inside him to make sure that didn't happen.

Just as Cassidy kicked the knife from the man's hands, two other men appeared from above.

The men had been hiding in the trees, just waiting for them to arrive.

She should have known.

In the blink of an eye, Colton had one of the guys in a headlock. Axel had knocked the other one out.

The third man still lay on the ground, searching for his knife.

She let out a breath.

Thank goodness Colton and Axel had been with her.

Wasting no time, they put zip ties on the men's wrists and stuffed rags into their mouths. They secured them to a low-hanging tree branch before proceeding toward the house.

Cassidy didn't think Ravi had any other men here. Based on what she knew, he only had a few with him. One of those guys had been beheaded.

Cassidy reached Chen and quickly checked his pulse.

He was still alive but unconscious. His bullet-proof vest had probably saved him.

Then she, Colton, and Axel carefully climbed the steps to the deck of the cottage.

Voices drifted from inside.

One in broken English.

Another voice was Ty's.

"It has to be this way," a female said.

Cassidy froze.

That was . . . Jasmine.

Wait . . . she was in on this?

Disgust roiled inside Cassidy.

How could that woman betray Ty like this? Especially after everything he'd done for her? Cassidy had known something was off about the entire situation.

Quickly, she darted toward the door and pressed herself against the wall.

Colton went to the other side of the door while Axel circled around back.

She peered through the window. Ty was sitting in a chair with zip ties holding his arms down.

Cassidy's throat went dry when she saw the knife the other man held. It was large . . . and sharp. Something dark stained the edges.

Was that blood?

Her head spun a moment.

Jasmine stood behind Ty with a gun, almost as if daring him to make a move.

Cassidy's resolve strengthened even more—if that was possible.

"In case I haven't mentioned it yet, I've been imagining doing this for a very long time. So I intend on enjoying myself." Ravi took the knife and ran it along Ty's throat, but he didn't break the skin.

Not yet.

Cassidy knew it was just a matter of time.

They could burst in there now. But Jasmine held that gun to Ty's back. All the woman had to do was pull the trigger, and Ty would be gone.

Cassidy couldn't let that happen.

She and her team would need to plan this carefully—but quickly.

She glanced at Colton. Based on the terse expression on his face, he felt the same apprehension.

One wrong move could be fatal.

"I'm going to need one slice of the knife for every day I've been without my bride," Ravi muttered. "Yes, it will be thousands of agonizing marks. You will beg me to finish. Beg me just to kill you. But I won't. Not until I'm ready. Not until you've suffered as I have suffered without my wife and son."

With those words, Ravi slashed his blade across Ty's bicep.

As Ty grunted, Cassidy's breath caught.

No!

She and her team had to act, and it had to be now.

TY FELT the blade tear into his skin and knew time was running out.

Ravi had to know that people would find him soon.

That's why when he felt the second and third slices, he knew his death would be painful but quick.

Ravi made another slice, this time on Ty's leg.

Ty already felt the blood saturating his clothing.

"Stop, Ravi. Please leave him alone!" Jasmine pleaded.

"You're nothing," Ravi spit out. "And no one. You can't tell me what to do!"

Jasmine let out a shaky sob behind him.

Ty couldn't let this go on any longer.

He swung his leg and kicked the knife out of Ravi's hand.

Then he ducked.

Just in time.

Jasmine pulled the trigger.

But the bullet missed him and hit Ravi instead.

As it did, the doors burst open.

Cassidy and Colton flooded into the front, and Axel came in from the back.

They surrounded Ravi and Jasmine, guns drawn.

But Ravi was already on the floor, clutching his knee where he'd been shot.

Colton quickly took the gun out of Jasmine's hands.

As soon as he did, she collapsed on the floor in a heap of sobs and despair.

"Where's Elijah?" Ty turned toward Ravi.

"Somewhere safe. Somewhere *she'll* never find him." He sneered at Jasmine.

Compassion washed through Ty.

One way or another, Ty would find Jasmine's son and make sure he was safe.

As Colton and Axel took charge of the scene, they cut Ty's arms loose, and he stood.

His gaze met Cassidy's.

The next instant, she holstered her gun and flew into his arms.

Despite the blood on his clothing, he pulled her close.

For a moment, he'd thought he might not be around for her future. For Faith's.

The mere thought had the power to crush him.

"I was so worried," Cassidy murmured in his ear.

"I know. I was too." He held on to her even more tightly.

Just then, numerous law enforcement vehicles surrounded the house.

There was going to be a lot of explaining to do.

Ty only hoped he could now put this part of his past behind him for good.

———

Cassidy didn't want to let Ty out of her sight. But right now, paramedics had to treat him while she answered pertinent questions from investigators.

Ty hadn't lost enough blood to be critical, but he had lost a lot.

Still, the whole situation had felt too close. Ty was still recovering from his other stab wound on top of these new injuries.

This whole confrontation . . . it could have been so much worse.

She was thankful Ty was alive. Prayers of gratitude kept rushing from her lips.

Donaldson had shown up along with the other three members of Chen's FBI team.

One of them, Agent Marco, had taken the lead, and Cassidy had explained to him how she'd found Chen on the ground. The man was still unconscious, but Ty had told them that Chen was the mole this whole time.

Marco hadn't seemed surprised.

Apparently, Donaldson had suspected that Chen might be dirty. He had checked the man's bank account, found a large deposit there, and put the facts together. Just this morning, he'd gotten confirmation about some secret trips Chen had recently taken. He was in the process of getting his superiors involved when he'd heard Ty was taken.

Cassidy wasn't sure what would happen to Jasmine. The woman had played a part of this, but she'd also been coerced. Cassidy had a feeling she'd get leniency in exchange for testifying against her husband.

Meanwhile, Ravi continued to spout lies and claim diplomatic immunity, even as the medics worked to stop the blood flow from his bullet wound.

Once the news media caught wind of Ravi's presence in the US, they'd be all over the story.

Ravi was a powerful dictator with terrorist ties,

and he had somehow managed to sneak into the country and had tried to kill multiple people. There was no way this ordeal could be covered up.

Cassidy wasn't sure exactly what that would mean.

All she knew was that for the most part, this was finally over. She could sleep better at night knowing that the situation was over.

But she was definitely going to take Ty up on that vacation he'd mentioned. They would bring Faith with them. Their little family needed some time away from this craziness—and Ty's parents could probably use some quiet time for themselves also.

As Cassidy finished talking to Agent Marco, she excused herself and walked over to the ambulance where Ty was being treated.

At one time in her life, she'd been content to be single. But now she couldn't imagine her future without Ty. God had brought him into her life, and Cassidy couldn't have found someone more perfect for her.

She grabbed his hand and raised it to her lips, planting a firm kiss there. "You gave me a good scare."

"I wasn't sure how things were going to turn out there for a moment either." He rocked his head to the side as if feeling an ache. His skin looked pale. His lip was busted. Bandages covered his arms and legs.

But he could heal from all those things.

"At least it's over." Cassidy's breath caught as a new thought hit her. "Unless . . ."

"Unless what?" Ty narrowed his eyes as he waited for her to finish.

"Are there any other people you've abducted in the past that might show up looking for you on Lantern Beach?"

"Sorry, I'm not at liberty to say." Ty shrugged and grinned. "It's classified."

Cassidy groaned.

These secrets from their past felt like too much at times. But they were expected in their current and past lines of work.

However, Cassidy prayed the situation with Jasmine and Ravi was the last secret she and Ty ever had to keep from each other.

CHAPTER
THIRTY-EIGHT

THE NEXT DAY, Cassidy looked up from her desk as someone knocked at her office door.

Sierra Davis stood there.

"Come in." Cassidy nodded to an empty chair across from her.

The animal rights activist lowered herself into the seat before turning to Cassidy. "I heard there was a lot of excitement here on the island yesterday."

"Yes, to say the least." Cassidy knew word had spread throughout the island, but she didn't want to get into those details with her visitor. Instead, she shifted in her seat and asked, "What brings you by?"

"I'm about to head back to Norfolk."

"Does that mean you're satisfied that everything is okay here?" For a moment, Cassidy prayed that Sierra knew something she didn't. That these dead fish were all just an act of nature. That trouble on the island had ebbed away with the tide.

"I still think something illegal may have happened, but I'm going to have to let the government handle it," Sierra said. "I heard that they're coming to town today, and I've already sent them all the information I've collected so they can make an informed decision."

"That's what I heard. I expect officials to be here at any time." Mac had been overseeing the situation while Cassidy had been dealing with Ravi Jabal.

"I tested those waters again just yesterday, and the levels of chemicals in them are clearing up some." Sierra pushed her glasses up higher on her nose. "That's to be expected since the substances potentially dumped in the marshes and surrounding waterways should be diluted by now. But that still doesn't mean that this incident is good for the environment or won't have long-reaching implications."

"I agree. I don't like what's going on, and I assure you that we'll be looking into this further."

"I'm glad to hear that. In the meantime, if I may say, you need to keep your eye on Ocean Essence. There's something going on there. Something fishy." Sierra made a face. "Excuse the pun."

Cassidy couldn't resist the smile that tugged at the corners of her mouth. "Excused. I'll definitely be watching them. If someone did something wrong, they'll have to face a penalty. Dumping chemicals is a serious matter with stiff penalties."

"I hope so. It's a shame that innocent creatures have to suffer for the sake of what's often referred to as 'progress.'"

"Agreed. Thank you again for your help."

Sierra stood with a resolute nod. "If you need anything else from me, please let me know. My best friend . . . well, she considers herself somewhat of a detective. So I've kind of gotten used to investigating things and fighting for justice."

"I'll keep that in mind. If there's anything else we need you for, I'll be in touch."

Only a few minutes after Sierra stepped out, Cassidy heard another knock at the door.

Had the woman forgotten something?

She glanced up, fully expecting to see Sierra again.

Instead, Ty stood there with something in his hands—straw hats.

"What are those for?" Cassidy raised an eyebrow as she eyed them. They weren't her normal fashion choice—Ty's either.

Ty grinned. "Just because?"

"That's a likely story."

He leaned close, placed one of the hats on her head, and planted a kiss on her lips. "Is it?"

As Ty settled across from her desk, Cassidy adjusted the hat and observed him a moment. She was so thankful her husband and best friend was okay.

He had more than thirty stitches, and he was taking an antibiotic to make sure infection didn't set in.

He'd be sore for a while, but overall, things could have been so much worse.

Cassidy let out a long breath, feeling herself relax just a little as she realized the whole ordeal with Jasmine was finally over. Now, they all just needed to recover and pick up the pieces.

"How's Beckett?" Cassidy asked.

"He should be coming home tomorrow."

"That's good news. What about Elijah? Have you heard anything else?" The boy had been abducted from Minnesota, so the case was out of Cassidy's jurisdiction. But she definitely wanted to keep tabs on it.

"As a matter of fact, I did hear something. Donaldson updated me and said that Ravi had the boy with him. Ravi and his crew were staying in a hunting lodge on a private island in the Pamlico Sound. Authorities found the boy there unharmed."

"That's great news." She'd been praying they'd find Elijah quickly and easily. The boy had already been through so much.

"His adoptive parents are on the way, but Jasmine is hoping to meet the boy herself. That will be up to his parents."

"As it should be," Cassidy said. "I'm glad he's okay."

"Me too."

She leaned back in her seat, the goofy hat still on her head—for the time being. "How did this whole situation even happen? How did Ravi find Jasmine? I'm still trying to wrap my mind around it."

Ty had been talking with authorities all morning, so Cassidy hoped he had an update.

"From what I understand, Ravi discovered Jasmine's location by utilizing some high-tech facial recognition software," Ty said. "Once he knew her location, he had one of his men leave a burner phone outside Jasmine's door. As soon as she found it and picked it up, the device rang, and she answered. It was Ravi."

"That's terrible."

"As soon as Jasmine realized Ravi had Elijah, she knew she'd do anything to get him away from Ravi. But Ravi already had someone on the inside—Chen."

"Why Chen?"

"Chen was in the army before joining the FBI. He was involved in an incident in Sahili—he accidentally killed a civilian. The Sahili army captured him and brought him before Ravi. Ravi promised to let him go if he would do his bidding. Chen agreed."

"It seems like you would have heard about that."

"Chen was only missing for two hours. When he was found, he was in the middle of nowhere and claimed to have lost his memory. The truth only came out last night. Anyway, Chen was able to use his connections and find out information on Jasmine. Then he began feeding information to one of the agents assigned to guard her."

"He was pretty determined, considering how classified that information was."

"Chen knew he'd go to jail for the rest of his life if he were discovered. He was in too deep. Since Ravi had been tracking Jasmine's internet searches, he knew she was researching me. He followed her when she fled, and he got his wish. She led him right to me. Ravi wanted us both in the same place."

"This could have turned out so much worse, Ty." She frowned as sadness pressed down on her.

He squeezed her hand. "I know. But it didn't."

"What secret was Donaldson hiding?"

"He had a feeling an FBI agent was dirty, but he

was trying to find out something definite before he told me. That's what he said, at least."

"So why was he so late getting here?" Cassidy still had more questions.

"Because he discovered Chen had been asking questions about Project Aladdin. Donaldson played dumb with me, but he already suspected someone with the bureau was involved. He knew the FBI had arrived in Lantern Beach, and he wanted to check out the agents who'd come out so he could know who to trust."

"The man is slightly off-putting, but maybe he did know what he was doing."

"So it appears."

She tapped her hat. "So what's this really for?"

"I've just booked a vacation at an all-inclusive resort in the Caribbean for you, me, and Faith. We're leaving in two days."

"Two days? But—"

"I've already talked to Mac. He approved a week-long vacation for you. Said it was overdue and that Bradshaw could be in charge."

Cassidy stared at him a minute before nodding slowly. "Okay then. That sounds great."

"You like that idea?"

"I more than like it. I love it!"

A grin spread across his face. "I was hoping you would."

Two days.

Things had been so unsteady lately, Cassidy couldn't wait to get away and plant her feet firmly on the ground—or rather, the sand—and make memories with the two people she loved most in the world.

~~~

Thanks for reading **Unsteady Ground**. If you enjoyed this book, please consider leaving a review.

Stayed tuned for *Troubled Graves*, coming next!

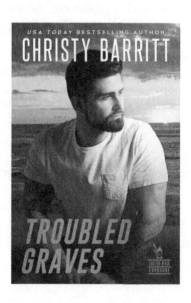

ALSO BY CHRISTY BARRITT:

BOOKS IN THE LANTERN BEACH UNIVERSE

LANTERN BEACH MYSTERIES

The series that started it all! When a notorious gang puts a bounty on Detective Cady Matthews' head, she has no choice but to hide until she can testify at trial. But her temporary home across the country on a remote North Carolina island isn't as peaceful as she initially thinks. Living under the new identity of Cassidy Livingston, she struggles to keep her investigative skills tucked away. One wrong move could lead to both her discovery and her demise.

#5 Perilous Riptide
#6 Deadly Undertow

LANTERN BEACH ROMANTIC SUSPENSE

Standalone romantic suspense novels that fear a pulse-pounding story centered around beloved Lantern Beach residents.

Tides of Deception
Shadow of Intrigue
Storm of Doubt
Winds of Danger
Rains of Remorse
Torrents of Fear

LANTERN BEACH PD

When a cult moves to Lantern Beach, the whole island is in upheaval. Police Chief Cassidy Chambers must find answers before total chaos erupts.

#1 On the Lookout
#2 Attempt to Locate
#3 First Degree Murder
#4 Dead on Arrival
#5 Plan of Action

LANTERN BEACH BLACKOUT

Join a group of Navy SEALs who've come to Lantern Beach to start a private security firm. But a secret from their past may destroy them.

#1 Dark Water
#2 Safe Harbor
#3 Ripple Effect
#4 Rising Tide

LANTERN BEACH GUARDIANS

During a turbulent storm, a child is found on the beach, washed up from the ocean. Making matters worse—the girl can't speak.

#1 Hide and Seek
#2 Shock and Awe
#3 Safe and Sound

LANTERN BEACH BLACKOUT: THE NEW RECRUITS

Four new recruits join Blackout, but someone is determined to teach them a lesson.

#1 Rocco

#2 Axel

#3 Beckett

#4 Gabe

LANTERN BEACH MAYDAY

Kenzie and Jimmy James work on a luxury yacht chartering a dangerous course.

#1 Run Aground

#2 Dead Reckoning

#3 Tipping Point

LANTERN BEACH CHRISTMAS

Catch up with your favorite Lantern Beach characters as they come together to help the town's beloved police chief.

Silent Night

LANTERN BEACH BLACKOUT: DANGER RISING

A new team is formed to combat a new enemy. The mission puts everyone on the line, and failure will mean certain death.

#1 Brandon
#2 Dylan
#3 Maddox
#4 Titus

BEACH BOUND
BOOKS AND BEANS MYSTERIES

When widow Tali Robinson moves to Lantern Beach to renovate an old oceanfront store and turn it into a bookstore/coffee shop, the last thing she expects to find is a human skeleton hidden within the walls. But her troubles don't stop there, and before long she realizes she doesn't have to dig for trouble, she's bound to run into it.

#1 Bound by Murder
#2 Bound by Disaster
#3 Bound by Mystery
#4 Bound by Trouble
#5 Bound by Mayhem

ABOUT THE AUTHOR

USA Today has called Christy Barritt's books "scary, funny, passionate, and quirky."

Christy writes both mystery and romantic suspense novels that are clean with underlying messages of faith. Her books have sold more than four million copies and have won the Daphne du Maurier Award for Excellence in Suspense and Mystery, have been twice nominated for the Romantic Times Reviewers' Choice Award, and have finaled for both a Carol Award and Foreword Magazine's Book of the Year.

She is married to her Prince Charming, a man who thinks she's hilarious—but only when she's not trying to be. Christy is a self-proclaimed klutz, an avid music lover who's known for spontaneously bursting into song, and a road trip aficionado.

When she's not working or spending time with her family, she enjoys singing, playing the guitar, and exploring small, unsuspecting towns where people have no idea how accident-prone she is.

Find Christy online at:
www.christybarritt.com
www.facebook.com/christybarritt
www.twitter.com/cbarritt

Sign up for Christy's newsletter to get information on all of her latest releases here: **www.christybarritt. com/newsletter-sign-up/**

facebook.com/AuthorChristyBarritt
twitter.com/christybarritt
instagram.com/cebarritt

COMPLETE BOOK LIST

Squeaky Clean Mysteries:

    #1 Hazardous Duty

    Half Witted (Squeaky Clean In Between Mysteries Book 1, novella)

    #2 Suspicious Minds

    #2.5 It Came Upon a Midnight Crime (novella)

    #3 Organized Grime

    #4 Dirty Deeds

    #5 The Scum of All Fears

    #6 To Love, Honor and Perish

    #7 Mucky Streak

    #8 Foul Play

    #9 Broom & Gloom

    #10 Dust and Obey

    #11 Thrill Squeaker

    #11.5 Swept Away (novella)

#12 Cunning Attractions

#13 Cold Case: Clean Getaway

#14 Cold Case: Clean Sweep

#15 Cold Case: Clean Break

#16 Cleans to an End

While You Were Sweeping, A Riley Thomas Spinoff

The Sierra Files:

#1 Pounced

#2 Hunted

#3 Pranced

#4 Rattled

The Gabby St. Claire Diaries (a Tween Mystery series):

#1 The Curtain Call Caper

#2 The Disappearing Dog Dilemma

#3 The Bungled Bike Burglaries

The Worst Detective Ever

#1 Ready to Fumble

#2 Reign of Error

#3 Safety in Blunders

#4 Join the Flub

#5 Blooper Freak

#6 Flaw Abiding Citizen

#7 Gaffe Out Loud

#8 Joke and Dagger

#9 Wreck the Halls

#10 Glitch and Famous

#11 Not on My Botch

Raven Remington

Relentless

Holly Anna Paladin Mysteries:

#1 Random Acts of Murder

#2 Random Acts of Deceit

#2.5 Random Acts of Scrooge

#3 Random Acts of Malice

#4 Random Acts of Greed

#5 Random Acts of Fraud

#6 Random Acts of Outrage

#7 Random Acts of Iniquity

Lantern Beach Mysteries

#1 Hidden Currents

#2 Flood Watch

#3 Storm Surge

#4 Dangerous Waters

#5 Perilous Riptide

#6 Deadly Undertow

Lantern Beach Romantic Suspense

#1 Tides of Deception

#2 Shadow of Intrigue

#3 Storm of Doubt

#4 Winds of Danger

#5 Rains of Remorse

#6 Torrents of Fear

Lantern Beach P.D.

#1 On the Lookout

#2 Attempt to Locate

#3 First Degree Murder

#4 Dead on Arrival

#5 Plan of Action

Lantern Beach Escape

Afterglow (a novelette)

Lantern Beach Blackout

#1 Dark Water

#2 Safe Harbor

#3 Ripple Effect

#4 Rising Tide

Lantern Beach Guardians

#1 Hide and Seek

#2 Shock and Awe

#3 Safe and Sound

Lantern Beach Blackout: The New Recruits

#1 Rocco

#2 Axel

#3 Beckett

#4 Gabe

Lantern Beach Mayday

#1 Run Aground

#2 Dead Reckoning

#3 Tipping Point

Lantern Beach Blackout: Danger Rising

#1 Brandon

#2 Dylan

#3 Maddox

#4 Titus

Lantern Beach Christmas

Silent Night

Crime á la Mode

#1 Dead Man's Float

#2 Milkshake Up

#3 Bomb Pop Threat

#4 Banana Split Personalities

Beach Bound Books and Beans Mysteries

#1 Bound by Murder

#2 Bound by Disaster

#3 Bound by Mystery

#4 Bound by Trouble

#5 Bound by Mayhem

Vanishing Ranch

#1 Forgotten Secrets

#2 Necessary Risk

#3 Risky Ambition

#4 Deadly Intent

#5 Lethal Betrayal

#6 High Stakes Deception

#7 Fatal Vendetta

#8 Troubled Tidings

#9 Narrow Escape

#10 Desperate Rescue

The Sidekick's Survival Guide

#1 The Art of Eavesdropping

#2 The Perks of Meddling

#3 The Exercise of Interfering

#4 The Practice of Prying

#5 The Skill of Snooping

#6 The Craft of Being Covert

Saltwater Cowboys

#1 Saltwater Cowboy

#2 Breakwater Protector

#3 Cape Corral Keeper

#4 Seagrass Secrets

#5 Driftwood Danger

#6 Unwavering Security

Beach House Mysteries

#1 The Cottage on Ghost Lane

#2 The Inn on Hanging Hill

#3 The House on Dagger Point

School of Hard Rocks Mysteries

#1 The Treble with Murder

#2 Crime Strikes a Chord

#3 Tone Death

Carolina Moon Series

#1 Home Before Dark

#2 Gone By Dark

#3 Wait Until Dark

#4 Light the Dark

#5 Taken By Dark

Suburban Sleuth Mysteries:

Death of the Couch Potato's Wife

Fog Lake Suspense:

#1 Edge of Peril

#2 Margin of Error

#3 Brink of Danger

#4 Line of Duty

#5 Legacy of Lies

#6 Secrets of Shame

#7 Refuge of Redemption

Cape Thomas Series:

#1 Dubiosity

#2 Disillusioned

#3 Distorted

Standalone Romantic Mystery:

The Good Girl

Suspense:

Imperfect

The Wrecking

Sweet Christmas Novella:

Home to Chestnut Grove

Standalone Romantic-Suspense:

Keeping Guard

The Last Target

Race Against Time

Ricochet

Key Witness

Lifeline

High-Stakes Holiday Reunion

Desperate Measures

Hidden Agenda

Mountain Hideaway

Dark Harbor

Shadow of Suspicion

The Baby Assignment

The Cradle Conspiracy

Trained to Defend

Mountain Survival

Dangerous Mountain Rescue

Nonfiction:

Characters in the Kitchen

Changed: True Stories of Finding God through Christian Music (out of print)

The Novel in Me: The Beginner's Guide to Writing and Publishing a Novel (out of print)

Made in the USA
Las Vegas, NV
11 December 2023

82540640R00184